The conversation around her came to a halt…and she saw him.

Jarrett, holding out his hand. "Can I have this dance?"

Are you sure that's a good idea? asked a voice in her head.

No, I'm not sure at all.

But as she placed her hand in his, a bad idea had never felt so good.

"I, um, haven't danced since the accident." But as his palm slid to her lower back and he pulled her body close to his, heat spread from his palm throughout her limbs, melting every bit of resistance within her.

He smiled. "Not a lot of call for dancing on the ranch, either. But I figure we make the perfect partners—you lean on me, I lean on you. As long as we keep our feet moving, we can call it dancing."

It was what a relationship was supposed to be, wasn't it? Two people trusting in one another.

She cupped the back of his neck, her fingers sliding into his hair, and she didn't feel the least bit clumsy. With the heat flaring in his eyes, the slight catch in his breath, she felt sexy, seductive…whole.

And she liked it.

THE PIRELLI BROTHERS:
These California boys know what love is all about!

Dear Reader,

While *Romancing the Rancher* is technically the fourth book in The Pirelli Brothers miniseries, for me, the books started with Sophia Pirelli, the Pirelli sister, in *Her Fill-in Fiancé* (July 2011). With Sophia's brothers finding happily-ever-after in books of their own, I thought now would be a good time to bring in another Pirelli girl.

Theresa Pirelli has spent her life caring for others. When an accident leaves her physically and emotionally traumatized, she travels to her cousins' hometown of Clearville, California, to rest and recover. Romance is the last thing on her mind, especially a romance with her temporary landlord, Jarrett Deeks.

Former rodeo star Jarrett Deeks knows a thing or two about rescuing horses, but rescuing a woman like Theresa isn't in his skill set. Even so, he finds himself drawn to the beautiful nurse. He's determined to put a spark back in her eyes...before she heads back to the big city where she belongs.

On the outside, Theresa and Jarrett might not have much in common, but inside they both have the caring and compassion to help each other heal.

I hope you enjoy *Romancing the Rancher* and look for more Pirelli Brothers stories to come!

Stacy Connelly

Romancing the Rancher

Stacy Connelly

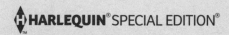

Recycling programs
for this product may
not exist in your area.

ISBN-13: 978-0-373-65863-3

Romancing the Rancher

This edition published by arrangement with Harlequin Books S.A.

For questions and comments about the quality of this book, please contact us at CustomerService@Harlequin.com.

® and TM are trademarks of Harlequin Enterprises Limited or its corporate affiliates. Trademarks indicated with ® are registered in the United States Patent and Trademark Office, the Canadian Intellectual Property Office and in other countries.

Printed in U.S.A.

Stacy Connelly has dreamed of publishing books since she was a kid, writing stories about a girl and her horse. Eventually, boys made it onto the page as she discovered a love of romance and the promise of happily-ever-after. When she is not lost in the land of make-believe, Stacy lives in Arizona with her three spoiled dogs. She loves to hear from readers at stacyconnelly@cox.net or stacyconnelly.com.

Books by Stacy Connelly

Harlequin Special Edition

The Pirelli Brothers

Small-Town Cinderella
Daddy Says, "I Do!"
Darcy and the Single Dad
Her Fill-In Fiancé

Temporary Boss...Forever Husband
The Wedding She Always Wanted
Once Upon A Wedding
All She Wants for Christmas

Visit the Author Profile page at Harlequin.com for more titles.

To the people who dedicate their lives
to animal rescue—my doggies and I thank you!

Chapter One

"You know, you're more than welcome to stay with us."

Theresa Pirelli shifted her gaze from the towering redwoods flashing by the passenger-side window to glance over at her cousin Sophia Cameron. Concern drew Sophia's dark eyebrows together beneath her fringe of bangs, and Theresa forced a smile.

A smile she'd gotten used to pulling out like fine china—all for show and, often she feared, just as fragile. "As much as I'd love to spend my whole trip spoiling that baby of yours, the three of you need your time alone."

And so do I.

After the weeks she'd spent in the hospital following a devastating car accident and then the months of recovery under her parents' watchful and worried eyes, Theresa desperately needed an escape. But it had to be one that wouldn't cause her parents further angst. A visit to Clearville and to meet the newest member of the family fulfilled both of those needs.

But with her cousin Drew getting married to local baker, Debbie Mattson, her family would soon descend en masse on the Northern California town. Her freedom from their almost suffocating concern wasn't going to last long, but she planned to make the most of it and use these precious days to figure out what to do with the rest of her life.

"Not so much alone time that you couldn't stay with us for a few weeks. Adult conversation is appreciated, you know. I'm half afraid baby talk is going to become my first language."

Despite the complaint, Theresa didn't think she'd ever seen her cousin so happy. And why not when Sophia was married to the man she loved. A man who was not her son's biological father. They'd had a rocky start to their relationship, but Jake had fought hard to prove that he was the family man she'd been looking for, finally winning Sophia over.

It was a similar battle to the one Theresa had fought with her fiancé, Michael Parrish. Only she had lost.

Her muscles tightened, as if physically trying to block out the memories. Her right hand curled into a tight fist in her lap while her left hand…did not.

After pulling in a deep breath, she made sure her voice was even and calm as she stated, "It's not like we won't see each other while I'm here just because I'm staying outside of town."

"I know but…in one of Jarrett Deeks's cabins?"

From what Theresa had read online, along with being an equine rescue, the Rockin' R offered trail rides, lessons and boarding for horses. Recent expansion included building half a dozen or so guest cabins on the property. Judging by the somewhat stark descriptions on the website, the cabins didn't offer much in the way of amenities. They were an alternative for people who didn't want to stay in the cute and cozy Victorian bed-and-breakfasts the small town was known for.

Theresa supposed hunters and fishermen drawn to the area by its rugged wilderness weren't interested in sleeping in the "Rose Suite" or "Daisy Drawing Room."

"I'm sure the cabins will be fine," Theresa insisted. Long hours working as a nurse in a St. Louis emergency room had taught her to sleep wherever and whenever she could. Lumpy couches, narrow, uncomfortable beds, even sitting on the floor with her back propped up against a wall had all provided her with a few hours' rest between many a shift.

All part of the job she loved. The job she lived for…

"I know the cabin will be fine," Sophia was saying, her cheerful voice calling Theresa back from the empty, endless void of her future, "but I was thinking that having you stay over would be like when we were kids, and you and your brothers used to come visit."

Memories of those long-ago summer vacations drifted through her thoughts. How she'd loved the freedom of roaming the woods outside her cousins' small hometown. "That's a nice thought," she told her cousin, even though she knew those carefree days were long gone. "But I need some time on my own."

She'd been offered a place to stay for the next month with any one of her four cousins, but Sophia and Jake had the new baby, Nick and Sam were both newly married, having met the loves of their lives within the past year, and Drew was preparing for his own wedding. Her aunt and uncle had also offered her a room at their home, but that would have been almost the same as staying with her parents.

Even the small apartment above the antiques shop Sophia managed on Main Street had been a little too close.

She could imagine family popping in every few hours. She loved them all and appreciated their concern—truly. But the strain of pretending everything was all right weighed so heavily on that porcelain facade, hairline cracks had started to show through. And just the thought of letting her family, or *anyone*, know how damaged she was beneath—

It won't happen. I will not *break.*

She unclenched her fist, covered her left hand with her right and ignored the voice in her head whispering that she was already broken.

A few minutes later, Sophia pulled the car to a stop in front of a rustic building at the end of a graded dirt road. Through the trees, Theresa could see a corral and what she assumed to be the stables. As she opened the car door, the early-spring air carried a faint hint of hay and horses. The surroundings were so peaceful and quiet, she took her first deep, relaxing breath since…she didn't know when.

"I'm pretty sure this is Jarrett's rental office," Sophia said as she rounded the front of the car and approached the building, "but it doesn't look like he's around."

"I received an email confirming my reservation, so I'm sure this Jarrett knows I'm coming." The website hadn't offered any information about Jarrett Deeks, the owner of the stables and the newly built cabins. Sophia had said something about the man being a retired rodeo star.

Theresa could easily picture the aged cowboy relaxing in one of the rocking chairs that sat on the small porch. The perfect spot to greet guests and tell tales about roping calves and riding bulls or whatever he'd done back in the good ole days.

"He's probably down at the stables," Sophia said with a frown.

"Then I'm sure he'll be back to the office in a few minutes."

Her cousin sighed. "From what Nick says, Jarrett can be totally fixated when it comes to his rescue horses."

Theresa knew the feeling. Or make that *had* known the feeling. The hectic pace of the emergency room could be overwhelming without the ability to focus on the job at hand. She could admire that kind of determination, and if it meant he'd forgotten about her arrival…well, that was okay.

She grabbed the edge of the car door to help pull herself to her feet, careful to balance her weight on her right leg. But even then, the muscles in her entire left side screamed after the long flight from St. Louis and ride in from the airport. The reconstructive surgeries on her knee had gone as well as expected, and thanks to the titanium rod and screws holding her broken femoral shaft together, the fracture had healed to a point where she no longer needed the crutches she'd so hated.

But the recovery was taking so much longer than she'd anticipated, even if her doctors and therapists insisted her rehabilitation for her leg was right on track. If she kept up with her therapy, she would in time regain her strength and range of motion. It was her other injury, the one far less obvious than the broken femur and damaged knee, that had a less-promising prognosis.

Nerve damage…

Could completely heal…

Might regain full use of hand…

But for all their noncommittal responses, Theresa feared her body was giving an answer that screamed louder than any words. The nerves *weren't* healing. She *didn't* have full use of her hand.

Look at you! You can't even take care of yourself. How do you expect to help anyone else?

Echoes of the harshly spoken words battered her, the emotional blow rocking balance and stealing her breath as much as the ache in her left leg. Theresa forced herself to move as if she could run from the painful memories, but the best she could manage was a shuffling walk that failed to outdistance any of the raw images from that final fight with Michael.

"Maybe we should drive down to the stables," Sophia was saying as Theresa made her way toward the porch.

The breeze cooled the sweat gathering at her hairline, and she was almost out of breath, but she'd made it from the gravel drive and up the three front steps. Waving a hand at one of the rockers, she said, "I'll just wait here for him."

"Theresa, no."

"Sophia, yes," she retorted. "I'll be fine."

The weather was crisp and cool, but far milder than the snowstorm she'd left behind in St. Louis. A small stream of sunlight filtered through the trees, bathing the corner of the porch with a warm glow. She'd brought her knee-length, red wool jacket and black leather gloves with her and would be perfectly warm enough to wait outside for Jarrett Deeks.

Between her time stuck in the hospital, in rehab and then at her parents' house, she didn't think she'd spent more than a few hours outside since the car accident. And most of that time was dedicated to the long, painful process of getting to and from doctors' appointments.

"I'll just get my bags and—"

But Sophia was already racing back toward the car with a cheery, "I've got them!"

And of course, she did. She had the wheeled suitcase and over-the-shoulder bag out of the trunk and back up on the porch before Theresa could have made her way down the front steps.

She pulled in a deep breath. After all, in the months since the accident, she'd learned a lot about patience, hadn't she? Swallowing the anger, the frustration, the self-pity at her inability to complete the simplest tasks from bathing to walking to putting on her own shoes. She'd come a long way, and she just needed to hold on to that patience a little while longer and wait for the rest of her family to catch up.

So she simply said, "Thank you," as her cousin set the luggage beside her.

Sophia beamed back and leaned in for a hug. "I'm so glad you're here."

Anger and frustration slipped away, and she was grinning by the time her cousin pulled back. "I am, too."

"What's so funny?"

"You still wear the same perfume, but you also smell like baby formula."

Sophia rolled her eyes. "It's the latest scent. Worn by exhausted new mothers everywhere."

But Sophia didn't look exhausted. With her dark hair cut in a short pixie style and her brown eyes sparkling, she looked as adorable as she had when they were kids and just as happy. Ignoring the twinge of jealousy, Theresa said, "You make it work. Now go back to that beautiful baby and hot husband of yours before he tracks you down like we both know he can."

"He is rather amazing, isn't he?" Sophia asked with a smile, but rapid blinking told Theresa she was fighting back tears. "He said he loved me enough for both of us and that it wouldn't matter..."

"But you still wondered," she filled in softly.

Her cousin shook her dark head. "I shouldn't have. Not even for a second."

"You're a lucky woman, but I still think if you asked him, Jake would say he's the fortunate one. He has you and your baby."

"Two for the price of one," Sophia joked. "Who doesn't love a bargain?"

After another few minutes arguing that Theresa would be fine waiting by herself until Jarrett Deeks arrived, Sophia finally—reluctantly—agreed. She backed away from the small office with a wave, and Theresa waited until the car was out of sight before slowly lowering her aching body into the rocking chair. The long trip and mini-reunion at Sophia's place had left her far more exhausted than she dared let on.

The chair swayed beneath her weight as her legs gave out, and she practically collapsed into the seat. She was glad Sophia had a man she could lean on, but past history had taught Theresa she was better off standing on her own—no matter how shaky she sometimes found the ground beneath her feet.

Jarrett Deeks swore beneath his breath as he heard the approaching sound of a car engine and the crunch of tires over the gravel lane leading past the stables. It could have been someone interested in boarding their horse at his place. Or maybe tourists wanting to take a late-afternoon ride on one of his many trail horses. Even a kind soul looking to adopt one of his rescue horses. Could have been. But he'd bet the ranch it wasn't.

No, he was pretty sure that car carried his first paying customer and guest to his new rental cabins. He snorted as he gave the gelding he'd been brushing a final pat. When he'd placed ads in hunting and fishing magazines, his plan had been to target men like himself. Guys who enjoyed nature and wildlife and were looking for an escape from city life. Not that Clearville offered much in the way of city life. But the small-town sense of community was almost worse than crowded cities and their towering sky-rises.

Getting lost in the city was almost as easy as getting lost in the wilderness. Both could leave a man feeling small and insignificant, a breath away from disappearing and never being found again. But in this small town—

He couldn't disappear if he tried. He'd hardly set foot on Main Street before half the townspeople seemed to know who he was while the other half was busy finding out. The instant curiosity and word of mouth had been a help, he had to admit, both to his rescue and to the stables. He didn't doubt that it would give his newest venture into the hospitality business a boost, too.

But that still didn't ease the uncertainty he felt about *welcoming* people onto his property. Though he'd lived much of his professional life in front of a crowd, he'd left that world behind. He had no interest in where-are-they-now stories showcasing him as a has-been bull rider.

The affinity he felt for the animals had given him a second lease on life when his rodeo career ended—when his fans, his friends, even the woman who claimed to love him disappeared from his life. He'd felt as lost as some of the horses and didn't know where he might have ended up if the rescue hadn't given him a new purpose.

His boots echoed on the concrete floor as he walked down the center aisle, a sense of pride filling him, as Silverbelle—his latest rescue—stuck her head over the top of a stall. Her long, graceful neck was extended as she looked for a treat. He handed her the piece of carrot he'd saved for her. She'd come a long way, and he was determined to keep the rescue going for other horses just like her.

That was where the idea for rental cabins came into

play. Cabins for hunters and fishermen. Outdoorsmen like him. Not so much for women. And sure as hell not for Theresa Pirelli.

What was she thinking, staying at the Rockin' R in the first place? If she didn't want to room with family, the bed-and-breakfasts in town were made for a woman like Theresa. Elegant, graceful and delicate, the beautiful buildings with their gorgeous gardens and what he assumed were lace-and-floral guest rooms would be a perfect backdrop for her.

Jarrett didn't doubt Theresa was very much a modern woman, but with her creamy skin, raven hair and blue eyes, she had an ethereal, timeless beauty. Seeing her at one of her cousins' weddings, he'd thought she looked like one of those cartoon princesses his half sister had loved as a kid—all big eyes, bright smiles and long, flowing hair.

She didn't belong in a rustic cabin unless seven dwarves were staying there with her.

Heaving a sigh, he headed out of the stables. As he stepped outside, he gazed out at the dense trees surrounding his property. He inhaled the scent of pine and a hint of ocean air almost as if he could breathe in the peace and quiet. He'd long ago figured out he was far better with animals than he was with people. But at the moment, people paid the bills.

Jarrett wasn't a fanciful man, but the life insurance policy his father had left him had been a final gift and, more than that, a kick in the butt from the great beyond. Without his father's investment in his future, it would have taken years if not decades before he would have had the cash or the land he needed to get the equine rescue up and running. Thanks to his dad, he now had both.

But buying the small ranch and refurbishing the stables had taken up a chunk of change already. Add to that the bills for hay and feed and veterinary services, and what he had left wouldn't last long. That was where the rental cabins came in. If he could make a success out of those, he'd feel better about taking on more animals.

Which meant welcoming Theresa Pirelli onto his property even if she didn't really belong there. He shoved his hands into the pockets of his denim jacket as he rounded the curve toward the small rental office cabin.

He immediately spotted Theresa sitting in a shaft of sunlight on the front porch. As he drew closer, he saw her eyes were closed, and he felt as though he'd been handed a slight reprieve. A minute or two to try to come up with some welcome-to-the-ranch spiel he should have thought of long before now.

On a second glance, he realized another reason to be glad Theresa's eyes were closed. It gave him a chance to take in the sight of her without letting his shock show. Her skin was pale, devoid of any healthy glow, and her dark hair, caught back in a low ponytail, was a stark contrast. Shadows haunted her eyes and made the hollows of her cheekbones more pronounced. Yet somehow, she was still beautiful enough to make his breath catch in his throat.

Cowboy boots weren't made for sneaking up on people, and her eyes flew open the minute his foot hit the first step. Her blue gaze widened and then widened some more as she took him in—from the hat shielding his face, to the checked shirt beneath his denim jacket, his faded jeans and the boots that had signaled his approach.

Realizing she didn't recognize him—and why should she when he made a habit of not standing out in a crowd?— he said, "I'm Jarrett Deeks."

"You— You're—" She frowned, her delicate eyebrows drawing together, before she shook her head. "Sorry. I just wasn't expecting…" Her voice trailed off without telling him what exactly she hadn't expected, and she said, "Theresa Pirelli. Nice to meet you."

He managed a quick nod, that welcome speech completely deserting him and leaving him feeling as awkward and out of his element as he probably looked. "Cabin's not far from here. I can bring the truck around—"

"If it's not far," she said with a lift to her chin, "why not walk?"

Because you look ready to fall over in a stiff breeze.

He knew better than to say the words out loud. He'd heard about the car accident Theresa had been in. Knew she was in town to attend yet another of her cousins' weddings. But he could see she was here for another reason— to recover. Maybe even to figure out where her life went from here.

If he'd been a man better with words—better with women than with horses—he might have tried to tell her he understood. That he knew what it was like when life threw you to the ground and stomped on you with bone-crushing hooves.

Instead, he gave her what little he could. "Sure. Let's walk."

He grabbed the two suitcases immediately. Theresa might have won the walk to the cabin, but no way was he going to let her struggle under the weight of that luggage, not even to salvage her pride.

"I can get those," she insisted.

"All part of the service," he injected, pleased with how smooth that sounded.

She frowned, and he readied himself for an argument, but her focus and frustration quickly turned toward the challenge of climbing from the low-slung rocking chair. She braced her feet on the porch and pushed off on the chair's upswing. She overcompensated for a weakness of her left side, and for a split second, he feared she'd fall.

Hands filled with luggage, he swore beneath his breath as she stumbled. He envisioned her hitting the porch the same time as the suitcases he dropped while reaching for her. His hands bracketed her upper arms, and his mind registered the thinness and fragility of muscle and bone even as his body breathed in a feminine scent of wildflowers.

Their gazes collided as she looked up at him. Her lips parted on a soundless gasp—pale pink, inviting and mere inches from his own. Close enough for him to feel a whisper of breath against his skin. Close enough to make him wonder—as he had ever since the first time he saw her—what it would be like to kiss Theresa Pirelli.

Chapter Two

She needed to seriously reconsider her definition of the word *retired*, Theresa thought, more shaken than she wanted to admit after the brief contact with the rugged cowboy.

Jarrett Deeks didn't speak with a Texas twang, and she could not for the life of her imagine him spinning tales for guests while sitting in one of the rocking chairs, whiling away the time as the world passed by.

Judging by the few lines bracketing either side of his mouth—she still hadn't gotten more than a shadowed look at his eyes thanks to the cowboy hat he wore—she figured him to be only a few years older than her own twenty-eight. He was young, virile, and exuded a barely restrained energy like a caged animal or maybe one of his horses, living for the chance to run free.

And she'd experienced a split second of that unleashed energy, hadn't she, when he reached out and grabbed her.

One moment he'd been by the porch steps, her bags in hand. In the next, he'd dropped her luggage, erased the distance between them and caught her in his arms.

And when he'd touched her—

She could still feel the heated imprint of his palms against her shoulders. Still feel that instant spark of attraction when hit with the awareness that Jarrett Deeks was not at all what she'd pictured.

She couldn't help glancing at him out of the corner of her eye as he led the way toward her cabin. He wasn't much taller than she was. His rugged profile, all masculine planes and angles from the nose that had clearly been broken more than once, to the sharp cheekbones and shadowed jaw, could have been carved from granite, and his leanly muscled body looked just as hard. Thick, chestnut-colored hair peeked out between the brim of his hat and denim collar, the only hint of softness about him.

She steeled herself against the warmth invading her body, threatening to melt even her uninjured muscles and bones. It was a weakness she couldn't allow. An overreaction to the first man in months to touch her without treatment or therapy or rehab in mind.

It was embarrassing, but she'd survive.

She should have realized *retired* did not necessarily mean *old*. She admittedly knew nothing about rodeo, but she did know about sports. Or more specifically sports injuries. She'd seen high school and college players come into the ER with everything from concussions to torn MCLs and ACLs to even more serious spinal injuries. A bad-enough injury could end an athlete's career at any age, and *retired* in the world of sports often meant anyone over thirty.

She should have realized— Heck, she should have asked Sophia! If she'd known he was someone her own age, maybe she would have been more prepared. Less caught off guard. Less…intrigued.

No, that wasn't true. She was not intrigued. Merely surprised. Jarrett Deeks was unexpected, but that did not make him a mystery she needed to solve. She had her own problems to deal with and a reticent, old-fashioned—if not old—cowboy was not on her to-do list.

Especially not when it was all too easy to resent how effortlessly he'd picked up her luggage, one bag slung loosely over a broad shoulder and her large suitcase dangling from his hand.

Before the accident, she'd never been a woman who insisted on doing things her own way. Oh, sure, she'd been perfectly capable of taking care of herself. She could change a tire and check her own oil. She could manage a few home maintenance repairs in her small apartment. But she'd appreciated when a man was a gentleman. When one opened a car door for her or waited for her to enter a restaurant ahead of him.

Michael had been good about that. Always insisting on picking up the check, buying her flowers and carrying her bags for her. After growing up with three brothers who, when they were kids, thought smaller and weaker meant easier to pick on, it was nice to be treated like a princess. As though she was someone to cherish and care for.

But since the accident—since Michael—the need to fight for every speck of independence was like a living thing clawing its way out from inside her. She wanted to snap at Jarrett Deeks for hauling her bags around so easily. To yell at him for the way he'd purposely slowed his stride. But the bitter truth of it was, she didn't have the energy or the breath to do any of those things.

Even with the solicitous crawl he'd established, she was already winded. The thought of carrying her own bags was a joke. She couldn't even carry a conversation, not that the silent man at her side had given any indication he wanted her to.

But after a minute with the only sound the crunch of gravel beneath their feet and whisper of wind in the pines, even he seemed to realize the silence had gone on too long. It only made his attempt to break it that much more awkward, but she gave him credit for trying as he told her about the property.

"There are six cabins total, but they're pretty spread out, and even if they weren't, you're the only guest right now. I figure your family will set you up with a pair of wheels if you want to run into town, but you can always borrow the ranch truck if you'd like. I've made a deal with the sporting goods store in town. You'll get a discount for any rental equipment you might need for hunting or fishing."

He couldn't have been much plainer about stating she didn't belong, but for some reason, his noncommittal statement made her smile. Hunting and fishing. Yeah, she'd get right on that.

But Jarrett's next offer wiped the grin right off her face.

"You're welcome to the stables, too—"

"I don't ride."

His steps slowed even more, bringing them almost to a halt, as he looked over at her. "The rides are based on ability—from advanced to greenhorn. I could show you—"

"Not interested. Sorry." Her abrupt words didn't let on just how sorry she was. She wasn't a greenhorn, as Jarrett had supposed, and had once taken a great deal of pleasure spending time in the saddle, even if her riding had mostly been limited to an indoor jumping arena.

She'd fallen in love with horses as a kid when her parents sent her to a summer camp that offered riding lessons.

One trip around a ring on an old gray mare that to her young, impressionable mind was as impressive as Black Beauty, the Black Stallion and Seabiscuit all rolled into one, and she was hooked. Her fascination with horses far outlived the two-week camp, and she'd pestered her parents until they found a riding stable just outside the city. Looking back, she was sure they thought her interest would fade once the summer ended and school started. Instead, the lessons had only been the beginning as Theresa progressed from learning to ride for fun as a kid to jumping in competitions during her high school years.

Now, though, riding was like too many other previous pleasures in her life—a reminder of all she could no longer do. No way could her left leg support her own weight to mount up from the proper side. She didn't need to try to know she didn't have the strength for that or the muscle tone needed to grip the saddle with her knees and thighs to keep her balance in the seat. And forget trying to hold on to the reins. One sudden move, and she'd be flat-faced in the dirt.

Oh, sure, Jarrett could probably saddle up some old, sweet-tempered mare whose gait would be as smooth as riding on a child's merry-go-round. But it wouldn't be the same. Wouldn't be the challenge, the thrill, the rush she'd experienced in the past.

And she'd rather do without than settle for so much less.

Fortunately, Jarrett didn't seem the least bit offended by her blunt refusal. If anything, Theresa thought the tension in his shoulders eased ever so slightly. He'd forced himself to make the offer and was relieved she hadn't accepted. Why? Because he honestly didn't think she could keep her seat on a horse and was worried about his first paying guest suing him? Or was it something more? Something to do with the air of reserve that fit him as well as the faded denim jacket stretched across his broad shoulders?

Didn't matter. He'd made the offer; she'd refused. End of story.

She ignored the slight shift in the wind, a change from the surrounding pine and distant hint of ocean air back to the hay and horses she'd smelled earlier. Both when sitting by herself on the porch and while caught in Jarrett's arms. His clothes held the earthy scent along with a masculine musk that had tempted her to burrow closer, to breathe deeper.

The thought of riding by his side, showing the former rodeo cowboy what a city girl could do, tortured her. She wasn't that girl anymore, and indulging in fantasy only made reality that much harder to accept.

Reality being a leg held together by pins and screws, a surgically repaired knee and nerve damage in her arm that left her full recovery—as well as her whole future—in doubt.

"Here's the cabin," Jarrett said as they rounded a bend in the narrow road and came across the small cabin. The rustic and rough-hewn logs blended in perfectly with the surrounding wilderness.

Jarrett fished a large key chain fashioned in a crooked *R* out of his pocket. A metal key was attached. He shouldered the door open, but then paused and waited for her to enter first. Despite her assurances to Sophia that she'd be fine, she breathed a small sigh of relief as she stepped inside.

"It isn't exactly a luxury suite," Jarrett said as he lowered her luggage and waved a hand around the small space. The kitchen was little more than a single row of cabinets, a stove, microwave and refrigerator, everything in basic white. A round table marked the dining room before giving way to the living area. A green love seat and matching chair sat in front of a flat-screen television with only a fireplace on the far wall to offer a little bit of coziness to the otherwise stark space.

"Bedroom and bath are down that hall. Again, nothing fancy."

"Try not to oversell the place," Theresa said wryly.

He shrugged. "Just being honest."

The three words almost sounded like an accusation... or a challenge. Almost as if he knew how hard she'd tried to dismiss that moment on the porch as nothing. But that was ridiculous because it had been nothing, and it wasn't as if the man could read her mind anyway!

"It's fine," she insisted shortly. "I'm not looking for fancy." She sensed rather than saw the way his gaze focused on her as she looked around the cabin, almost as if he was questioning what she was looking for. "Just a spot to relax and the chance to enjoy some peace and quiet."

He made a small sound that might have been a laugh. "Peace and quiet, huh? This is a funny place to come for that considering you're related to half the town."

"I can count on my family to respect my privacy."

Theresa turned and met his shadowed gaze. For a crazy moment, thoughts of what the two of them could do with that privacy filled her head. The not-fancy bedroom was just down the hall, and even though she had yet to see inside, she could count on there being a bed.

Her whole life, she'd played things safe. She'd known early on what she wanted from life—to become a nurse and work in an ER—and had followed through with the plan she'd set to accomplish that goal. She'd studied hard and worked hard, and she never let distractions get in her way. If she were totally honest, even her relationship with Michael had been a step toward a personal goal—one to get married and start a family.

And yet for all her careful planning, for all the steps she'd taken in the right direction, she'd still ended up here. Miles away from Michael, from her work, from her life, knowing all too well how unlikely it was she would ever get any of them back.

Here. In this cabin with an all-too-sexy cowboy.

She could still feel the imprint of his hands against her shoulders, the warmth and strength that had seeped through in that simple, straightforward touch. Her heart skipped a beat, and her pulse pounded in her ears, and for the first time in longer than she could remember, it wasn't because she'd pushed too hard in therapy or because she'd taken an awkward step only to catch herself before falling. And it wasn't from the panic attacks that had woken her more than once as she faced an empty, aimless future.

No, this—this was something else.

This was attraction...desire.

And while that cowboy hat of his might have shielded his expression, it hadn't been enough to hide what he'd been thinking in that split second when he held her in his arms. He'd wanted to kiss her. She'd seen it in his eyes as he'd lowered his gaze. Felt it in the tightening of the muscles that played beneath the palms of her hands. Wanted it more than she'd wanted anything in a long time.

But she'd seen something else, too, hadn't she?

Because Jarrett Deeks hadn't simply pulled her into his arms. No, she'd practically fallen at his feet, and the idea that she might have mistaken pity for something more doused her heated thoughts faster than an ice bath.

Her voice was sharper than she intended when she said, "My family will give me the privacy I'm looking for. I trust that I can expect you to do the same."

A small smile quirked his lips, and the lines around his mouth deepened though the expression was more sardonic than sincere. He tipped the hat Theresa found herself wishing he'd taken off. She wanted to know what color his eyes were. Brown to match the richness of his hair? Blue for the open skies above or green for the surrounding pines?

She didn't have the chance to find out. Backing out of the door, he said, "Peace and quiet are just what these cabins offer. I'll be sure to let you enjoy yours."

He was gone before she knew it, leaving her alone as she'd requested, and she was an idiot for feeling disappointed at just how quickly he'd walked away.

As it turned out, Jarrett Deeks knew her family a little better than she did.

Theresa was still wiping sleep from her eyes and contemplating the apparent lack of a coffee machine—never mind actual coffee—when she heard the knock on her door. Her foolish, utterly feminine heart jumped before her far more practical brain reminded her that Jarrett Deeks had better things to do than offer her room service.

Or breakfast in bed, she thought, surprised when her thoughts actually went there with images of Jarrett Deeks still wearing that darned hat and little else.

She was pathetic. There was no other word for it. For her body, an instrument that had caused her nothing but pain and misery for months, to suddenly come alive thanks to a man who was so wrong for her seemed almost as big a betrayal as her current weakness did.

Shoving the thoughts aside, Theresa opened the front door.

"I know you said you wanted some time alone," Sophia said by way of apology, "but I'm here with a special delivery."

"So I see," Theresa said with a smile. How could she

be angry when her cousin was holding her adorable baby boy in her arms?

Sophia laughed. "Actually, I wasn't talking about this guy, but he is pretty special if I do say so myself." She lifted the blanketed baby a little higher, and Theresa got a glimpse of a sweet round face, sleepy blue eyes and a tuft of dark hair. Kyle scrunched his face up in protest as the cool air touched his chubby cheeks, and she didn't think she'd ever seen a more adorable sight.

"Oh, he's awake." He'd been sleeping the day before, and Theresa had only had a peek of him slumbering away in his crib.

"He just about fell asleep on the way over here, and I promise we won't stay. But I was talking with my mother, and she was worried about you being up here without any food—you know how she thinks food cures everything. Anyway, she wanted to race over and cook enough meals to last your whole trip, but I convinced her I could bring out some leftovers and groceries to tide you over until you felt like running into town."

"Thanks. I woke up this morning realizing I hadn't really thought that part of this trip through." And having to seek out Jarrett Deeks after her bitchy stand about wanting her privacy…well, she'd rather go without breakfast than have to eat crow.

"Oh, you're welcome. Now, if you'll just hold Kyle for a second while I run to the car and get everything…"

"No, Sophia. I—I can't!" Theresa took an immediate step back as her cousin held out her son. A tiny, helpless infant.

A part of her longed to cradle the baby to her chest, to breathe in the newborn's scent of milk and baby powder. But the idea of holding that life in her hands, of being responsible if something should go wrong— Unconsciously, she drew her left arm closer to her body. "It's not a good idea."

Sympathy and understanding filled her cousin's gaze. "I trust you, Theresa. You know that, don't you?"

It had taken Michael months before he'd trusted Theresa with his daughter, and that had been a horrible mistake. The car accident hadn't been her fault, but his blame and Theresa's own overwhelming sense of guilt weighed her down as heavily as if she'd been the one to run the red light.

"I'll get the groceries," she insisted and escaped from the small cabin before Sophia could protest. Broken eggs she could handle much more easily than broken bones and broken lives.

"This is nice," Sophia said as she glanced around the cabin once they'd settled in at the small kitchen table for a cup of coffee and a shared strawberry Danish from Debbie's bakery. She held her son so easily, so naturally in one arm, and true to his mother's earlier words, little Kyle had fallen into an innocent, trusting sleep. "I knew with Drew being involved in the construction that the workmanship on the cabins would be to his usual high standard, but Jarrett did a lot of the finish work himself."

"Really?" Theresa asked, only to immediately wish she hadn't sounded so interested. "I mean, I wouldn't have thought a former bull rider turned ranch owner would be all that handy when it came to construction."

The spark in her cousin's eyes only deepened, and Theresa snapped her mouth shut so fast, her teeth clicked together. *Way to overexplain.* The last thing she wanted was for Sophia to pick up on her unwanted attraction to Jarrett Deeks.

Recalling her shock at her first glimpse of the man in

question, Theresa said, "You could have warned me, you know. From what I'd heard about Jarrett, I was expecting this old guy and not someone—"

"Someone so gorgeous?" her cousin filled in.

"Someone so *young*, that's all. I was just surprised."

"You've got to watch him at work, Theresa. I had to stop by the stables to ask which cabin was yours and saw him with one of his horses. It's...breathtaking."

"So says the happily married woman."

"Yes, to her gorgeous and single cousin."

Theresa rolled her eyes. "Yeah, well, don't pin your matchmaking hopes on me and Jarrett Deeks."

Or on me and anyone else.

Her heart was still reeling from her breakup with Michael. The car crash had shattered nearly everything in her life—personally, professionally...and emotionally. When she first woke in the hospital, her first thoughts had been of Michael—and of his daughter, Natalie. She'd loved them both and wanted to be there for them in any way that she could. Just as she'd needed Michael to be there for her. She'd counted on him being there. Instead, he'd walked away.

Now that she'd gotten back on her own two feet physically, Theresa wasn't about to start leaning on another man. Wasn't about to trust one again. And no matter what crazy emotions Jarrett might have inspired in her the day before, without trust, those heated thoughts would stay in fantasyland, where they belonged. At least until she could find a way to get the man off her mind altogether.

"I was not matchmaking," Sophia insisted. "Merely commenting that you and Jarrett have something in common. I know how much you like to ride."

"Liked," Theresa stressed. "Past tense." When her cousin would have argued, she continued, "Besides, Jarrett and I didn't exactly get off on the right foot, so I think we'll both just keep our distance."

Sophia frowned. "That doesn't sound like Jarrett. I mean, he doesn't talk much, but I've never known him to say something inappropriate—"

"No, it wasn't anything like that." Theresa wished she'd kept her mouth shut, but now that she'd stuck her foot in it, she was going to have to explain. She couldn't let Sophia think Jarrett had done something wrong when he hadn't. "He was just being polite in offering to show me around the stables, but I'm not interested. I told him I want to be left alone, and it came out a little sharper than I intended."

"So you'll go down and apologize and ask him to give you the grand tour."

"Sophia—"

"Look, I meant what I said about Jarrett being a good guy, but he's not exactly the type to make an offer like that simply to be *polite*."

"No, he did it because the stables are one of the perks of staying here." She was a guest and nothing more. Theresa didn't want to think that his offer may have been a personal one.

"If you say so," Sophia answered in a singsong voice.

"I do." And whatever it took, she was going to force herself to believe it.

Chapter Three

"Um, no."

Make that hell no, Jarrett thought as Nick Pirelli dogged his heels as he walked down the narrow aisle of the stables. The local veterinarian had offered his services as soon as Jarrett started the rescue operation, and a part of him had been waiting for this moment. Well, not exactly for this moment, he thought, still feeling the jolt of surprise at the request, but for the moment when the other man would call in his chips.

Oh, sure, Nick had told him pro bono work was something he did on a regular basis. That he respected the rehabilitation Jarrett did with the rescue horses and wanted to be a part of it. But Jarrett had learned long ago that nothing in life was free, and once you owed another person, they *owned* you.

So he insisted on paying for the vet's services, though he suspected the bills were greatly deflated from what Nick would normally charge, and the year before he'd taken on an abandoned horse as a favor to the other man. Not that he would have turned the horse away under any circumstances, but it'd been a way to try to even the score.

His muscles were tight, his movements jerky as he stripped off his scarred leather work gloves while he waited for Nick to turn his request into a demand. He was the only large-animal vet in the area, and they both damn well knew it. Jarrett couldn't run the rescue or the ranch without Nick's services, and that dependency—that need—to rely on another person twisted his gut. How many times had life slapped him down with the lesson that the only person he could count on was himself?

"Look, Jarrett," Nick began, and Jarrett braced himself for the ultimatum he knew was coming. *Do this or the horses suffer.* "I know it's a big favor to ask, but I'd really appreciate it."

Stuffing the gloves into his back pocket, Jarrett met the other man's gaze and waited. Then waited some more. That was it? Just the simple request? No blunt demand… no subtle insinuation of what might happen if Jarrett didn't fall in line?

The realization had him slowly lowering his guard. Truth was, he admired the work Nick did. Their love of animals gave them a common ground and was enough for Jarrett to think he might be able to call the other man friend. And friends did do favors for each other.

But not this. Pretty much anything but what Nick had asked.

"I know Theresa seems like she's doing okay."

Jarrett sighed. "That's what she wants you to think. Truth is she's far from okay."

He'd seen the pain in her expression when she thought he wasn't watching. Seen how hard she'd pushed herself just to make the easy walk to the cabin. Pride kept her from showing how weak she truly was, but he recognized the signs. Hell, he'd seen them more often than not whenever he looked in the mirror. If that was all that was going on with Theresa, then maybe he'd think about what Nick was asking of him.

He'd still say no. But he'd at least think about it first.

"Which is why I need your help," Nick pressed.

"But she's also a grown woman," Jarrett added, refusing to let his mind go where it wanted to go after those words. He didn't need to be thinking how womanly Theresa was while talking to her overprotective cousin. "And she needs to prove she can take care of herself while she works things out. Which is why she's staying out here. Which is why the answer is still no."

No, he was not going to look in on Nick's cousin. No, he was not going to go out of his way to make sure she was eating right and taking care of herself. No, he was not going to make another offer to take her riding or to show her around the property.

He planned on making that as clear to Nick as Theresa had made her disinterest in Jarrett's offer clear to him.

Okay, so for a second, he thought he'd felt an answering spark of attraction when he'd caught her in his arms on the porch. Maybe he had; maybe he hadn't. Either way, it didn't matter when the woman came straight out and said she wasn't interested.

Fine by him.

The last time she'd come to town, for Nick's wedding, she'd brought her boyfriend along. A surgeon from the hospital where she worked in St. Louis. Theresa had a type— blond-haired, blue-eyed, educated and wealthy.

And it didn't matter, he told himself *again*, that Theresa hadn't brought him along with her on this trip. He didn't want to know if she'd given the good doctor the same I-need-my-space speech or if the other man's absence had something to do with the sorrow Jarrett had seen in her eyes.

Theresa was not there for him to rescue.

Stopping in front of one of the stalls, he reached out and ran a hand down Silverbelle's forelock. The small mare stood passively beneath his touch, her soft brown eyes watching him with a hint of caution. Not long ago, the once abused and neglected animal wouldn't have let him come within ten feet of her. Her first few weeks in the rescue, he'd left her loose in one of the corrals, not wanting to traumatize her further by trying to force her into a stall. It had taken time and patience, not to mention decent food and fresh water, to help bring the horse around.

Jarrett was always amazed by an animal's ability to forgive, to move beyond the cruel treatment by humans in the past, and by their willingness to trust again.

Silver tossed her head and dislodged his hand from her warm and smooth hide, letting him know she'd had enough. She'd come so far, but that didn't mean he didn't still have work to do. She was still a little wary, a little standoffish—

Another pair of haunted eyes came to mind. A gorgeous blue instead of soulful brown.

And that was the real reason he wanted to stay away from Theresa. Her injuries went deeper than the physical damage done by the car accident. He could see the lingering shadows in her wounded gaze. Sadness, guilt, loss—he wasn't sure what swirled in the blue depths. All he knew was that he'd felt the pull sucking him in like a whirlpool when it'd be best for both of them for him to stay away.

Healing a horse's broken spirit—that he could do. Healing a woman—no. Not in his skill set. "Look, Nick, I'd like to help—"

"Great," the vet interrupted, showing off that I'm-older-and-therefore-know-better judgment he was known for. "I knew I could count on you."

But Jarrett had faced down one-ton bulls. He didn't let anyone run roughshod over him. "Like to," he stressed, "but I can't. I'm not the guy for the job. Trust me on this, okay?"

"I'm not asking you to date her. Just check in on her once in a while."

Jarrett clenched his back teeth. Not asking him to date her. Why? Did Nick think Jarrett wasn't good enough for his cousin? Just because he wasn't some fancy doctor or— He swore beneath his breath. What the hell did he care what Nick thought? He didn't even want to date Theresa!

He stopped outside Duke's stall, and the black horse shook his huge head with a short whinny—almost as if reading his thoughts and having a good old laugh. The gelding had technically been Jarrett's first rescue, but he knew better. The one-time cutting horse had been his salvation.

"Fine." He turned to face Nick. "I'll look in on her, but that's all. And if she tells me—again—to leave her alone, I'll be sure to let her know it was your idea."

"Now, wait a second." Catching sight of the look Jarrett shot him, Nick raised his hands. "All right, all right. It's a deal. We're just…worried about her, you know?"

Suddenly, the past few years disappeared in a blink, and Jarrett flashed back to the hospital room where he'd landed after a wicked toss from a bull. A lonely hospital room. What would it be like, he wondered, to have family surround you when you needed them most?

The thought reminded him of the message his half sister had left on his cell phone the other day, but he shoved it aside. Too bad he couldn't delete the memory as easily as he'd deleted the message. Summer wanted to come to California to help him with the rental cabins. He gave a silent snort of laughter. In his family, any offer of help always came with strings attached, and he was glad he'd cut all ties years ago—even if his half sister refused to accept that.

Theresa was lucky to have people around who cared about her for no other reason than the love they felt.

"I know. But your sister was here to bring Theresa groceries right after she arrived," Jarrett pointed out. "And then Drew and Debbie stopped by yesterday."

He couldn't complain too much about their arrival when Debbie, the local baker, had brought along a dozen to-die-for chocolate cupcakes and assured him Theresa wouldn't mind sharing. Which only meant Debbie gave him one of the miniature cakes. It did not mean Theresa would feed him with her slender fingers or that he'd get a chance to taste the rich, decadent chocolate straight from her lips— two images that had sprung to mind at the innocent comment.

"So?" Nick asked defensively enough for Jarrett to know he was well aware of where this was heading.

"So, if your cousin came here to have some time by herself, maybe you should give it to her and quit…hovering. You know as well as I do that the worst thing you can do with a skittish animal is hem her in."

The other man's scowl deepened into a glower. "My cousin is not a skittish animal."

Yeah, Theresa probably wouldn't think much of the comparison, either, Jarrett thought wryly. "All the more reason why I shouldn't be the one looking out for her."

* * *

Self-discovery, Theresa decided as she gazed at her reflection in the foggy medicine cabinet mirror hanging above the bathroom sink, sucked.

For all her talk about alone time and needing the opportunity to focus on what she wanted for the future, so far she'd come to only two conclusions. One, she didn't really like being by herself. And two, all she wanted for her future was the life she'd had in the past.

She hadn't expected staying alone at the cabin to be such a big deal. After all, she lived by herself. After a rough shift at the ER dealing with doctors, other nurses and patients, surrounded by a cacophony of sound—phones, pagers, voices over the intercoms, the beep of various monitors— by the end of the day, all she wanted was to go home and wrap herself in the peace and quiet of her cozy apartment. To enjoy the sweet relief from the stress and fast pace of the outside world.

Here, there was no outside world. At least, not a world Theresa was familiar with. She glanced at the window above the tub. Blue skies peeked through the softly swaying pines. Outside, the peace and quiet of the cabin was nothing but…more peace and quiet. So much of both that she was ready to scream. Just to give herself a break from it all.

And the sorriest part, she thought as she hit her wet, shoulder-length hair with the warmth of the blow-dryer, was that in the three days since she'd arrived, some member or another of her extended family had dropped by to visit, the most recent being her aunt and uncle.

They had shown up with the explanation that they wanted Theresa to have a vehicle while she was staying in the cabin. She was grateful even if she didn't have anywhere to go, and the need to escape only increased the longer her aunt and uncle stayed.

Her uncle Vince was a younger, slightly mellower version of her father. Both men were dedicated to their families, friends and neighbors. But just like whenever her father looked at her, Theresa could sense the concern behind her uncle's dark gaze. At least the older men in her family were the type to worry in silence. Not so much with her mother—or her aunt.

Vanessa had hovered over Theresa during the entire visit. How was she feeling? Was she sleeping all right? Did she have enough to eat? Was she keeping up with her exercises every day? Was she pushing herself too hard?

All that was bad enough. Worse were the questions she couldn't answer.

"What are your plans for when you go back to work? Your mother says you have an opportunity to go back to school for a career in hospital administration. Do you think you'll start classes soon?"

Following the accident, Theresa had been put on medical leave. That time would be up soon, and although she would be able to get an extension, she wondered what would be the point. Would a few more weeks make a big enough difference for her to be back to normal?

She shut off the blow-dryer and ran a brush through her hair. She caught the thick mass to one side and automatically reached up to start a simple braid, but the dark strands slid through the stiff fingers of her left hand. Sucking in a deep breath, she tried again. And again, and again.

She'd learned to braid her hair when she was seven years old and now—

Frustration tightened her body, and she clenched her jaw to hold back the urge to swear, to scream, to cry. Normal? Yeah, she didn't think so, and clearly her mother didn't, either.

Tossing her hairbrush back into the vanity drawer with more force than necessary, she left her hair loose around her shoulders and stepped into the bedroom to finish dressing.

Donna Pirelli had never been thrilled with her only daughter's career choice. Oh, she was proud that Theresa was a nurse, but she'd never liked the idea of Theresa working the long shifts in a downtown St. Louis hospital. The atmosphere in the emergency room was undeniably stressful, with people brought in after car accidents or medical emergencies like heart attacks or strokes. And then there were the other patients—victims of gunshot wounds or stabbings, not to mention drunks and drug addicts so out of their minds they were a danger to themselves—and to others.

So, yes, Theresa understood why her mother would prefer her to have a desk job dealing with policy and procedure rather than patients. And she told her aunt the same thing she always told her mother. "I'm still thinking about it."

Thinking how much she hated the very idea.

And just like her mother, her aunt hadn't been satisfied with that answer. Fortunately, her uncle had taken the hint and had reminded his wife that they needed to get back to town.

She'd felt both grateful and guilty when they left—an awkward combination of feelings she was almost getting used to when it came to her family. But while their leaving meant she didn't have to answer any more questions about her future, it didn't mean the questions went away. If anything, they only sounded louder in the small cabin's overwhelming silence.

"I have got to get out of here," she muttered as she sank onto the bed and shoved her feet into a pair of already-tied tennis shoes to go with her worn jeans and St. Louis Cardinals sweatshirt.

Jarrett had meant what he said when he told her the bedroom and bath weren't fancy. The furnishings were obviously new—from the queen-size bed with its neutral beige comforter to the matching oak nightstand and build-it-yourself dresser. But the stark walls and *emptiness* of the place were driving her crazy.

He'd also kept his promise to leave her alone, making her apology impossible to give.

She carefully pushed off the bed. One wrong move could still send white-hot bolts of pain shooting up and down her left leg, and she held her breath as she waited for the pull and protest of the weakened muscles. Was it wishful thinking or was the tightness easing just a little? She'd been keeping up with her exercises within the bare walls of the cabin, but a walk would do even more good, she decided as she left the car keys on the kitchen counter and stepped onto the porch.

It had rained sometime during the night, the fresh scent lingering in the damp morning air. Clouds hovered over the peaks of the distant mountains. Drops of rainwater clung to the pines and sparkled in the filtered sunlight. Sophia was right about the gorgeous scenery, Theresa thought as she walked carefully along the muddy pathway. Jarrett Deeks had picked a prime spot for his business.

She had the sudden thought that his choice hadn't been so much a professional one as a personal one. This land was the perfect place for *him*. A little rugged, a little wild...a little lonely.

A small shiver raced down Theresa's spine even as she scolded herself for ascribing attributes to a man she didn't even know. She was letting her imagination get away with her. She was used to dealing with men, from doctors to physical therapists to orderlies. Not to mention her three brothers. Granted, Jarrett didn't fit into any of those molds, but that hardly mattered.

Cowboy or cardiac surgeon, Jarrett Deeks was still just a guy, she reminded herself as she followed a path that led toward the stables. An ordinary, average—

Her thoughts, her entire body, came to a stop as she caught sight of the cowboy astride a gray horse in the middle of the corral. Her heart stumbled in her chest as she watched him circle the animal one way and then the other. Horse and rider worked as one, every movement fluid, effortless…and breathtaking.

Her pulse picked up its pace as she watched, the beat echoing the thunder of the pounding hooves against the hard ground. For a split second, Theresa swore she could almost feel the warm horseflesh beneath her, the rush of speed and excitement, of the cold air making her cheeks sting and her eyes water. The connection of horse and rider…

Or was it something else she was feeling? Something more?

Theresa wasn't sure when it happened, but she suddenly realized Jarrett knew she was watching. He did nothing to acknowledge her presence. Didn't dip the brim of his hat, didn't lift a gloved hand in a wave. All his concentration, his entire being, was focused on the horse. And yet there was this…awareness like an electrical current thrumming between them, drawing her closer despite the "Danger— High Voltage!" signs plastered all around.

He knew she was watching—and knew just what watching him was doing to her.

Theresa swallowed hard against a suddenly dry throat.

She didn't even remember moving—and since the accident, that was certainly saying something—but before long, her hands were braced on the cold metal railing circling the corral. Vibrations trembled along the crossbar as Jarrett galloped by, and Theresa again experienced the breathless sensation of riding alongside him.

Gradually, he slowed the pace, but the horse was still breathing heavily when he came to a stop in front of her. Beneath the brim of his cowboy hat, his cheeks were ruddy from the cold and wind, and his chest rose and fell from the exertion and exhilaration of the ride. Swinging a muscled leg over the horse's broad back, he dropped to the ground. His stride was steady and sure, but Theresa felt her own legs go weak as he approached.

He didn't stop until he'd braced his hands on either side of hers, and Theresa had the inane thought that a fence meant to hold half a ton of horseflesh couldn't come close to containing a man like Jarrett Deeks.

His deep voice scraped across raw nerve endings, and she couldn't suppress a telltale shiver as he murmured, "Change your mind about that ride?"

Chapter Four

Jarrett didn't know how many people he'd performed in front of during his days in the rodeo. From country fairs to packed arenas, he'd played to the crowd in the minutes leading up to the moment when he entered the chute. After that, everything disappeared. The sound of cheers, the scent of fried food from the concession stands, the burst of light from cameras flashing around him. All of it faded into nothing.

His focus narrowed to the bull he was determined to ride. Didn't matter if a hundred thousand people filled the seats or if the stadium was empty of a single soul. Only after he hit the ground—hopefully on two feet— did he once again become aware of the screaming fans all around him.

Even then, he'd never been cognizant of a single pair of eyes watching his every move. Never felt the warmth of a look as strongly as a touch.

But damn it if that wasn't how he'd felt with Theresa's blue eyes on him. It was as if her gaze had wrapped around him like slender arms, and she was seated astride the horse behind him. He shrugged his shoulders as if he could throw off the sensation of her body pressed against his back, but it didn't do any good. Not when she was standing in front of him, those eyes still focused on his.

"So…" he said, his voice sounding as gravelly as the road leading out to his place. "'Bout that ride…"

"Uh, no. Thank you."

He swallowed a deep exhale of relief. He'd known she'd turn him down, but there was still a brief moment of— What? Hope? More like sheer insanity if he'd wanted, even for a split second, for her to say yes.

Soft pink highlighted her cheeks, either from the cold or something he'd best not contemplate, and her gaze cut away from his to Silverbelle standing calmly on the far side of the corral. He was lucky the mare had come as far as she had. If he'd tried riding her a few weeks ago and let his concentration slip as he had today, he probably would have ended up landing on his ass in the dirt. And wouldn't that have given Theresa something to see?

"I wanted to tell you that I'm sorry for the other day. I was rude, and I apologize." Her gaze came back to meet his as she spoke, and Jarrett was hit by her sense of integrity and strength. She might look like a fairy-tale heroine, but Theresa had a toughness her beauty couldn't hide.

Of course, right in that moment, she didn't exactly fit the princess mold. She was dressed as casually as he was in jeans and a faded-to-orange sweatshirt. Her hair was loose around her shoulders, a few strands blowing across her cheeks thanks to the morning breeze, her face free of makeup. But just like the toughness that was so much a part of her, so, too, was the beauty and grace that had nothing to do with what she wore and everything to do with who she was.

"You weren't rude. You said what you wanted and—" he shrugged "—you're the guest."

"And the guest is always right?" A hint of disbelief lifted her words, but Jarrett wasn't sure what she was questioning. His words or the very idea that he thought of her as nothing but a guest.

"Company policy," he lied.

"Uh-huh."

"So how's all that peace and quiet treating you?" he asked before whistling for Silverbelle.

"I'm guessing you already know that my entire family has been out to visit me."

"Yep." Jarrett reached for the reins and started leading Silver toward the gate. On the other side of the fence, Theresa followed along. "So much for your alone time."

She gave a soft laugh. "You're pretty much the only one who paid any attention to that."

Jarrett shot a sidelong glance at her elegant profile. If he didn't know better, he'd almost think she was complaining. He swallowed a snort of laughter. His imagination had to be working some serious overtime to even come up with such a harebrained notion.

"They mean well," she said defensively enough to let Jarrett know she hadn't really minded their interruptions.

He shoved aside any thought that maybe he should have stopped by unannounced, too.

Opening the gate, he led Silverbelle through. By the time he had the latch secured behind him and turned around, Theresa was standing almost eye to eye with the horse. A protest rose in his throat when she reached up, but instinct held the words back. His breath caught in his chest as he waited to see what happened. He wasn't sure what interested him more—the horse's response...or the woman's.

Thercsa moved slowly, her voice a low murmur as she talked to the mare. If he hadn't seen for himself just how shy and nervous Silverbelle could still be, he would never have known it by her reaction to Theresa's gentle greeting. The horse lowered her large head as if seeking out closer contact as Theresa stroked a hand over the horse's muzzle.

So much for his theory that Theresa had rejected his offer to take her riding because she was afraid of horses. So was it because she was afraid of him? Afraid of whatever the hell it was he'd felt while she'd watched him ride? Had she felt it, too?

"She's beautiful," Theresa said softly. "What's her name?"

"Silverbelle. Silver for short. And you'll want to be careful around her," he said, well aware that his warning was coming too late and hardly seemed necessary. "She's a rescue and can be kinda shy."

"Oh, I had no idea. After seeing you ride together, I assumed she was one of yours."

"She is for now, and she's come a long way. Can't say yet that she'll ever be comfortable enough for trail rides or for riding lessons, but maybe." He shot her a sidelong glance as the three of them started walking toward the stables. "Speaking of trail rides—"

"No, thank you." Theresa crossed her arms over her chest. "I appreciate the offer, but I...can't."

Jarrett nodded, keeping his gaze straight ahead, but he couldn't pretend he hadn't noticed the way she cradled her left arm close to her body, tucking it beneath the right. He swore beneath his breath. He should have realized her reluctance might have been because of the injuries she'd sustained. But she'd pushed so hard to prove herself by walking to the cabin and then coming down to the stables that he hadn't given it a thought.

Instead, he'd shoved the offer for horseback riding in her face—not once, not twice, but a damned three times. And he was the man Nick wanted to look out for his cousin? He'd been right to shoot the veterinarian down.

"I could still use your help with the horses," Jarrett blurted out.

"I'm sorry, Jarrett, really, but—"

"You don't have to ride," he said as they reached the stables. "Just give me a hand with Silverbelle's tack and brushing her down. You're good with her, and she needs to learn that I'm not the only human she can trust."

"You really think that will help?"

Longing filled her blue gaze as she looked at Silver. The same longing he'd sensed earlier as she'd watched him in the corral. The phantom memory of her body pressed against his taunted him, but he forced it aside. This wasn't about the way Theresa made him feel. This was about putting the missing spark back in her eyes.

He was going to get her back in the saddle, Jarrett vowed. He didn't know how, and he had just over three weeks to figure it out, but he was determined to see Theresa ride.

Theresa wanted to say no. She really did. To spend time around Jarrett's horses, knowing she might never ride again—at least not the way she had before—would be its own form of torture. Just stepping inside the cool stables brought back too many memories. The building wasn't as fancy as the riding stables back home, but the scent of horses and hay, the sound of metal shoes on concrete, were all the same.

And then there was being around the man himself—an

entirely different kind of torture. He'd taken off his hat, and for the first time, she had the full view of his thick brown hair, cut short to the sides but with just enough length on top to make her fingertips tingle with the urge to touch. His face was as sculpted as his jawline with a wide forehead, eyebrows a shade darker than his hair and sharp cheekbones.

And his eyes… Not brown or blue or green, but a mix of hazel that combined all those colors into a piercing gaze that seemed to see right inside her.

A shiver raced down her spine, leaving goose bumps in its wake. What was it about Jarrett that made her body come alive? After the accident, she'd pretty much given up on feeling any spark of attraction or desire, too emotionally devastated by Michael's desertion and too physically compromised to experience those feelings again. And she'd been perfectly fine with that numbness.

So to come here and feel the rush of desire now—the weakness in her knees, the catch in her breath, the flush in her cheeks—all because Jarrett Deeks happened to glance her way… It was humiliating at the least. Slightly terrifying at the most.

She opened her mouth to refuse his offer when Silver nudged her shoulder. The mare's soulful brown eyes watched her closely, and Theresa knew it was only her own turmoil that made the animal's expression seem wary and yet hopeful. Yes, it would be hard spending time around the horses, but if she could help, wouldn't that be worth it?

"She's looking for a treat," Jarrett explained, though she didn't know how he even knew what the horse was doing when he was busy unbuckling the saddle. He'd hung up his denim jacket when they first stepped into the stables, and the soft cotton of the navy blue long-sleeved T-shirt he wore beneath stretched across his broad back and shoulders, defining every muscle.

Theresa jerked her gaze away, just in case he was as aware of her as he was of the horse. Keeping her eyes on Silver, she asked, "What kind of treat?"

"Just about anything edible." He lifted the heavy tooled leather as if it weighed nothing and carried it into the tack room. When he returned, he held a small plastic bag filled with apple slices. "Apples and carrots are her favorites."

Reaching inside the bag he offered, Theresa pulled out a piece of apple. She couldn't help but smile as the mare delicately nibbled it from her palm. She'd just reached for another slice when a horse in the stall beside her stuck out its large head and tried to snatch the apple right from her hand.

"Whoa, there, Duke! Ladies first!" Jarrett said as he stepped between Theresa and the other horse. "Sorry about that. This guy can be a little pushy when it comes to treats."

"Well, if that's the case, then I guess I'm a pushover," Theresa joked as she gave the horse a bite of apple. "You said his name is Duke?"

Jarrett nodded. "He was my first rescue," he said with a fondness that reached inside Theresa's chest and squeezed. A slight grin curved his lips, the faint expression lighting his stern features so much that she found herself longing to see him smile, to hear him laugh.

"Hard to believe he was ever shy," she said.

"He wasn't that kind of a rescue. Duke was a champion cutting horse back in the day. Won a lot of money over the years. People, crowds, none of that bothered Duke. Loved it, didn't you, boy?" Reaching up, he gave the side of the horse's neck a firm pat. "But after a while, age and some minor injuries started to catch up with him, and his owner, the kind of guy who sees his horses as money-makers, wanted to get rid of him."

"So you bought him."

"Yep. This guy's still got a lot of life in him. He still loves going out for a ride, and he's great for giving lessons 'cause there's nothing that'll spook him. He can't do everything he used to, but in a way, he's figured out how to do even more."

Theresa shot him a sharp glance. Was that his way of telling her she needed to move on, too? To finding her own something *more* now that working in the ER was a thing of the past? With all of her relatives coming and going over the past few days, it was impossible to believe one of them hadn't filled Jarrett in about her accident and her injuries.

Did he really think it would be that easy? To give up on the dream of a lifetime and find something else to do? Something as fulfilling, as challenging, as rewarding as the career she'd dreamed of since she was a child?

Frustration, loss and anger boiled up inside her. "Are we still talking about horses?"

"What else?" he asked laconically. Refusing to rise to her challenge, to admit what she knew to be true.

Theresa met his gaze as if by staring him down, she could force him to give a different answer. But with no more ammunition to fuel the fire, her anger started to wane. Maybe she was being too sensitive and reading more than she should into his words…

She didn't know how long the staring contest would have lasted if not for some outside interference. Tired of waiting for another treat, Duke nudged her shoulder. Hard. The unexpected contact knocked her off balance and right into Jarrett's arms. Her face burned at the first moment of contact. For the second time in as many meetings, she was practically falling at Jarrett's feet. And she'd worried about him feeling sorry for her before. Nothing like going back for another round of humiliation.

She quickly braced her hands between them, ready to push away, when the softness of the shirt he wore and the heat of the skin beneath seeped into her palms. Her heart began to race, but the rapid beat was nothing compared to the wild pounding within Jarrett's chest. She was close enough to feel the warmth of his breath against the side of her neck. If she turned her face, even a little, she'd feel the rough scrape of his day-old beard against her cheek. And if she turned just a little more, she would feel the heated press of his mouth against hers.

Their ragged breathing seemed to fill the stable, so much louder than the stomp of a shoed foot, the gusty blow of a nearby horse, the jangle of Silverbelle's bridle. But not so loud that Theresa didn't jump when she heard a vehicle door slam shut. Jarrett stepped back so quickly, reaching for the reins, that she almost wondered if she hadn't imagined the whole world-stopped-moving moment. Wondered if it wouldn't be better if she *had* imagined it.

"Excuse me a minute. I'm expecting someone." He quickly stabled Silverbelle and was striding toward the sliding doors before Theresa had a chance to catch her breath.

Reaching out, she placed a hand against Duke's neck, taking comfort in his solid warmth. She didn't think it was imagination that the horse rolled his eyes at her. "I know, right?" she murmured. "It's crazy, and I should totally know better. But don't think I've forgotten that this was your fault."

Despite her words, she carefully bent toward the ground, scooped up the baggie Jarrett had dropped and offered the horse the last slice. Apples might be on Duke's menu, but forbidden fruit? That was definitely off Theresa's.

* * *

She waited for a few minutes inside the stable, but when it became clear that Jarrett wasn't coming back anytime soon, Theresa gave Duke and Silverbelle a few farewell pats and headed for the door. She stepped outside in time to see Jarrett lead a pretty palomino out of a trailer.

Standing beside a dual-cab truck, a silver-haired man wrapped an arm around a blonde teenager. The girl rested her head against the man's denim-clad shoulder, wiping tears from her cheeks. The man Theresa assumed to be her father looked almost as heartbroken.

"Promise you'll find her a good home," the girl said to Jarrett, her words made no less strong by the dampness in her eyes or the tremor in her voice.

"We'd really like to keep her," the man added. "But I've been out of work for a while now, and the boarding stable in Redfield keeps raising its prices—"

"I told you I'd get a job. I could pay for feed and boarding, Dad," the teen argued.

"And if you're going to class during the day and working nights and weekends, when will you have any time for riding?" Heaving a sigh, the father gentled his voice as he added, "We talked about this, Chloe. Lightning deserves better than that. She deserves someone who has the time and the money to spend on her."

With his focus on the horse—running his hands down her back, over her flank, down her legs to her hooves— Jarrett didn't appear to have paid any attention to the father-daughter exchange. He'd moved to the horse's head before he asked, "You said you've been boarding her?"

"Yes," the daughter answered. "At a stable the next town over."

"So you just ride her for fun, then? And let the stable hands care for her the rest of the time?"

The girl straightened away from her father, drawing up to her full height. A sudden breeze whipped her hair across her face, and her pale eyes were flashing as she said, "I take care of her. I ride her *every day* after school. I spend hours at the stables on the weekends."

Theresa knew it was none of her business, but she took a few steps forward anyway. She couldn't blame Jarrett for centering on the horse, but if he'd take a look at the girl, he'd see how devastated she was to be giving up the animal she loved. Theresa had never owned a horse, though she'd begged for one almost constantly as a child. Her parents had wisely refused for the reasons Chloe's father mentioned.

She'd taken lessons when she could, and there had been times when she'd had to stop because of a lack of time and money. She'd been heartbroken, too, and could only imagine how much more painful it would have been if she'd not only had to give up riding but also give up her own horse.

Would it really be so hard for Jarrett to reassure the poor girl? To promise to find the horse a good home? To show a little understanding instead of asking questions that were only making her feel worse?

Theresa opened her mouth, ready to demand a moment of his time, when Jarrett gave the horse a final pat and finally turned his attention to Chloe. "You ever ride her bareback?"

"Of course."

He waved toward the corral behind them. "Mount up."

"What? Why?"

"I want to see how she responds to a rider she's familiar with."

Chloe met his unyielding gaze with as much confusion as Theresa was feeling. Was this his way of giving Chloe a chance to say goodbye? A last ride before she and her father turned their truck around and hauled an empty trailer back home? The teen seemed to come to that same conclusion.

Walking up to the horse, the girl ran a hand down its neck and murmured something for only the animal to hear. Then she pulled herself up with remarkable ease and agility. The wide gate squeaked as Jarrett swung it open and Chloe guided the horse through. Inside, the two raced around the ring—Chloe's long blond hair almost the same color as the horse's trailing mane.

They rode well together—beautifully and bittersweet— as a final farewell. And while Theresa was touched watching the two of them, the pulse-pounding connection she'd felt earlier wasn't there. Shooting a quick glance at Jarrett standing impassively a few feet away—his arms crossed and booted feet plated wide apart—she wasn't surprised. The experience hadn't simply been about watching a horse and rider. It had been watching *Jarrett* ride.

A few moments later, Chloe pulled Lightning to a stop and swung from the horse's back. She guided the animal over to Jarrett and seemed resigned, if not ready, to hand the reins over to him. "She's a great horse," the girl said a little defiantly as if challenging Jarrett to disagree.

But he merely nodded. "If you're still interested in looking for a job, I could use a hand around here. As the weather warms up, more people are going to be looking for trail rides and lessons. What you make should cover boarding and leave you with a little extra."

As his words sank in, pure joy lit her eyes. "You mean, I could work here and I could board Lightning and I—"

A half laugh, half sob cut off the rest of her words. And if the look on Chloe's face wasn't priceless enough, Theresa was gifted with the sight of Jarrett's pained expression when the girl threw her arms around him in a grateful hug.

Chapter Five

"That was nice of you."

Jarrett gritted his teeth as Theresa fell into step beside him as he led Lightning into the stable that would be the palomino's new home. A few of the other horses craned their necks out of the stalls, eyeing the newest arrival with curiosity and a whinny or two of greeting. Though he may have pretended to, he hadn't forgotten for a moment that she'd been there the whole time he'd talked with Chloe and her father. Not that her presence had affected his decision.

When the O'Malleys had called the day before, he'd known giving up the horse would be tough on the girl and maybe not the best thing for either one of them. He hadn't brought up the idea of hiring Chloe at the time because, well, he hadn't thought of it yet.

Even if he had, he would have needed to take a look at Lightning as well as see if Chloe could actually handle herself around horses. In the end, the situation made sense and had nothing to do with the weight of Theresa's stare or how knowing she was watching made him feel like a heartless jerk, robbing some poor girl of her horse. But still, he hadn't made the offer because of Theresa.

Especially not if it made her think he was nice.

"Look, it was a business decision. I'm trying to finish up work on the cabins and get that side of the operation up and running. That means I have less time for trail rides and lessons—even though that's what's bringing in the money right now. I've needed more help around here for a while, and it just makes sense to hire Chloe."

The majority of the students who came for lessons were young girls who, sometimes, loved the idea of horses better than the reality of sitting on a large animal several feet above the ground. He knew from his phone call with her father that Chloe had younger siblings. She'd be someone the female students could relate to and she'd be a hell of a lot more comfortable with a bunch of little girls than he was.

"So what you're saying is that you didn't do it to be nice," Theresa surmised.

"Exactly."

"Uh-huh." Her lips curved into a smile, and that moment before the O'Malleys arrived rushed back. That split second when it had taken every ounce of self-discipline not to crush Theresa in his arms, to feel every inch of her delicate curves pressed against him as he claimed her mouth with his own.

Jerking his gaze away, he focused on settling Lightning into her new stall, an easy enough task with the good-tempered mare. The horse stepped inside, her hooves crunching on the fresh straw as she took in her new surroundings. As he closed the stall door, he flinched a little, thinking of Chloe's promise to return and bring the engraved plaque with Lightning's name on it to adorn the front of the stall.

The girl's eyes had glowed as she said, "I was going to keep it, you know, as a memento, but now it'll be right on her door where it belongs so that she'll know that she's home."

He hoped Chloe didn't have anything else in mind to help the horse feel welcome. He could just imagine the stall covered in flowers and draped in girlie fabrics.

Judging by the hint of smile Theresa was unsuccessfully trying to hide, she knew what he was thinking. And wasn't that one damn scary idea? Because while he was as eager to throw off Chloe's gratitude as an ornery bull to shake off a rider, the warmth in Theresa's gaze made him feel...he didn't know what. But he knew for sure letting himself get pulled into that blue flame was a surefire way to get burned.

"It's no big deal," he ground out.

"Tell that to Chloe and her father," Theresa countered gently.

The ringtone on his phone interrupted the moment, and he reached into the back pocket of his jeans with relief. He didn't need Theresa thinking he was some kind of hero. Not when he knew the truth. When it came to being there when a person needed him most, he was nothing but a failure.

The phone call saved him from the rush of unwanted memories, but the minute he heard the sweet, Southern drawl, he cringed.

Talk about trading the frying pan for the fire. But at least Summer was on the other side of the country, unlike Theresa, who, despite his words, was gazing at him with a softness in her blue eyes that made half of him want to grab her by the shoulders and shake some sense into her while the other half—

Hell, that part of him just wanted to grab hold of her and not let go.

"Well, it's about time you picked up your phone. I suppose it's too much to ask for you to return one of my messages."

"That would mean having something to say."

His half sister sighed. "J.T.—"

"Don't call me that." The childhood nickname—like his brief childhood in Atlanta, like his family—were things he'd left behind long ago.

After a slight pause, his sister murmured, "Sorry, Jarrett."

His hand tightened on the phone. Truth was, he had no issue with his half sister and no reason for acting like such a jerk. "That's just...not who I am."

Her voice was wistful as she replied, "It's how I remember you."

It amazed him somewhat that Summer remembered him at all. Or at least that she remembered him fondly. The eight-year age difference had always struck him as huge. Most of his memories of Summer were of a crying baby, an annoying toddler and a spoiled child. Even if his memories were accurate, Summer had only been ten when he stopped going to Atlanta, fulfilling the regular, court-mandated visits.

That had been over a decade ago, and if he'd missed most of her bratty teenage years, he'd also missed her turning into a bright, beautiful—if stubborn—young woman.

Still, he argued, "You'd be better off forgetting."

"How can I?" Some of that bright, stubborn streak showed in her relentlessly cheerful tone. "You're my big brother."

"Summer—"

"I think it's awesome that you've started the rescue, and I don't know why you won't let me visit. You know I'm good with horses and love to ride. I could be a big help."

"Forget it." Even if he believed her, his half sister's offer came with big strings attached to his stepfather's fat wallet. And Jarrett refused to take a single penny from the man for the rescue or the ranch.

"Oh, all right." Summer huffed but gave up easier than he'd expected—and without the usual attempt to try to get him to reconcile with their mother. "But we'll talk later, okay?"

The eagerness in her voice made him feel like a heel, so what else could he say? "Yeah, okay."

Still, he couldn't help feeling as if he'd opened a rusty, rotting can of worms just with that simple agreement. Slipping the phone back into his pocket, he turned to see that Theresa had wandered a few feet away to pet Duke. Far enough not be intrusive, but not so far, he was willing to bet, that she hadn't overheard every word.

She didn't bother to deny it as their gazes met. "Demanding girlfriend?" she asked, a faintly mocking tone entering her voice.

"Half sister." He blurted out the truth before he had time to stop and consider that he might be better off letting Theresa believe he had a girlfriend. Or seven.

"Oh." Faint color highlighted her cheeks as she seemed to realize what she'd given away.

Jarrett fought the urge to let loose a curse. Bad enough having to deal with his own attraction. Add in the awareness that the desire he felt wasn't one-sided, and he wondered why they were even fighting what was already starting to feel inevitable. The reasons were there, but he wasn't thinking of them as he moved close enough to smell the spring-flower scent of her shampoo, close enough to see the subtle rise in her chest as she breathed and hear the catch in her throat.

"So, you, um, you and your sister aren't close?"

Jarrett abruptly reared back. That was a quick enough way to douse the heated moment between them. Talking about his family— He made it a point not to talk about them. Or *to* them as best he could manage.

If only Summer would take the hint.

"Half sister," he corrected. "And that depends."

"On what?"

"On whether you're asking me or asking Summer," he said wryly. "But no," he added when he saw the question still lingering in Theresa's gaze. "We're not close."

"Oh." There was that word again. Only this time instead of being accompanied by a charming and attractive blush, a puzzled frown pulled at her dark eyebrows. As if she couldn't imagine someone *not* being close to family.

Just another way their lives differed. Just another reason to keep his distance.

She couldn't figure him out.

Over the next few days, Theresa tried her best to remind herself it wasn't her job to try. She wasn't staying at the cabin to solve the mystery of Jarrett Deeks. If anything, her fascination was likely some form of transference. She didn't want to think about the problems in her own life, so her mind instead focused on the complicated former rodeo star. He was a good-looking distraction, and she was a sucker to let herself get pulled in.

Not that he'd done anything to encourage her. Just the opposite. Following the phone conversation she'd overheard— or more accurately, shamelessly eavesdropped on—she'd tried to get Jarrett to open up about his sister. But other than his initial comment that the two of them weren't close, he hadn't said a word.

Not close. Theresa supposed that was putting things mildly considering the change she'd seen come over him while he talked on the phone. The calm and ease he displayed with the horses disappeared. Tension had pulled at his shoulders, straightened his spine and tightened his expression into a remote mask. Even his voice had changed, flattened, as if his normal tone might reveal too much.

For some reason, as she watched him, she'd thought of the kids who were brought into the emergency room. Oh, sure, some of them were screamers determined to let everyone know how unhappy they were with whatever injury or illnesses had landed them there. But other children screwed their eyelids shut and kept as still and silent as possible, almost disappearing into themselves, as if that could make the pain go away.

"Not your business," Theresa muttered beneath her breath as she walked toward the stables. She shoved her hands into the pockets of her hoodie sweatshirt, her tennis shoes crunching on the dirt path. She wasn't there to heal Jarrett Deeks, whatever his wounds might be.

Pulling in a deep breath of the cool, pine-scented air as the building came into view between the trees, she took a quick inventory of her vital signs. Her pulse was elevated, but only slightly, and she didn't feel nearly as winded as she had just a day or two before. Each time she walked to and from the cabin, the trip seemed easier. Maybe it was simply that enough time had passed since the accident for her to start regaining strength. Maybe it was just the increased activity that kept her muscles from tightening up.

Either way, she couldn't deny that Jarrett was helping *her*.

Along with the physical activity, Theresa had incorporated some of her therapy into her work at the stables. Using her left hand to brush the horses or feed them a slice or two of apple, trying to encourage the damaged nerves to work again. It was far easier, she decided, to practice the simple movements for the horses' benefit than for her therapist, who watched with a trained, assessing gaze, or in front of her family, who couldn't keep their concern from showing. The animals didn't care how many times the brush awkwardly slipped from her hand or how many attempts it took to pick up a single apple slice—though Duke had tried to help her out by stealing the fruit straight from the plastic bag.

Her steps slowed as she neared the stables and caught sight of Jarrett with a new arrival. Unlike the first time she'd seen him at work, racing Silverbelle around the circle, this morning he and his latest rescue were both simply milling about in the corral. Or at least that was how it appeared until she eased close enough to hear the low rumble of Jarrett's voice. She was too far away to hear more than an indistinct murmur, but the words didn't matter.

The horse's ears flickered, its gaze still wary while tracking Jarrett's movements. For the longest time, the stalemate seemed unbreakable. But Jarrett never hurried, never pushed for more. Even from across the paddock, she could see the ease in his body language, lulling the horse—lulling *her*—into a relaxed state. She could feel her guard lowering and that sense of attraction growing.

Jarrett's quiet confidence was about the sexiest thing she'd ever seen. Her mouth quickly went dry, and she forced herself to swallow as she watched the masculine grace in his broad shoulders, leanly muscled arms and denim-clad legs. He was dressed the same as every time she'd seen him—jeans, a button-down shirt and his tan

Stetson riding low on his forehead. The typical uniform of cowboys and country guys all over, and yet she couldn't imagine it fitting another man better.

The brim of his hat hid most of his features, but that only added an air of mystery. And besides, she already knew just how handsome his rugged face was with his wide brow, deep-set eyes and stubborn, beard-shadowed jaw.

She'd pictured that face far too many times over the past several days.

Her breath caught as the horse took a sudden step, not moving away but walking toward the man in the corral. She had to stop herself from taking that same step, freezing in place as she watched the horse duck its head and take a piece of carrot from Jarrett's palm. He ran his free hand down the length of the horse's neck, and Theresa felt goose bumps race over her skin. If Jarrett turned that easy charm on her, she had no doubt she'd be eating out of his hand in no time, too.

Then as quickly as the moment happened, it was over. The horse tossed its head and retreated to the other side of the corral, and Jarrett sauntered away, both willing to pretend nothing momentous had just taken place. But Theresa wasn't fooled. She knew how hard that first step could be.

She braced her weakened knees as he turned toward her, half wishing she could blame the noodly muscles on the accident. Her pulse picked up its pace as he closed the gate behind him and headed her way. "Morning."

"H-hi." Theresa cleared her voice of the embarrassing catch in her throat and tried again. "How's she coming along?"

Jarrett glanced over his shoulder at the mare. "Just fine. She'll need another few days, but after that, I expect she'll settle in."

"Chloe told me she has another riding lesson this afternoon." The girl's enthusiasm for horses was infectious, erasing all of Theresa's misgivings about spending time at the stables. Instead of serving as a reminder of all that she couldn't do, her time was filled with dozens of little tasks that she *could* manage. Chores needed to be done, and she honestly didn't know how Jarrett had handled it all himself before hiring the teenager.

"After yesterday, today should be a piece of cake."

Theresa laughed at Jarrett's wry tone. Yesterday he'd catered to an eight-year-old's birthday party—half a dozen little girls with far more excitement and enthusiasm than ability. Which wouldn't have been so bad if that lack hadn't included an inability to pay attention. Within the first few minutes, the group had scattered—some racing toward the corral, others toward the stables and a shier few hanging back with the harried mothers who'd driven them.

Theresa hadn't known what to expect from Jarrett. Sheer panic had been one guess. Irritation another. Instead, with a somewhat resigned sigh, he'd asked Chloe to supervise the girls who'd taken off for the stables while he kept an eye and made sure none of the others slipped through the bars and into the corral. He ignored the timid ones—at least at first.

Like with his horses, he seemed to understand the kids needed time to explore at their own pace, some galloping full speed around the paddock, while others were afraid to leave the trailer. Eventually, though, he made his way over to the shy little girls. He held out a bag of sliced apples, letting them each take two—one to eat and the other to feed to one of the horses.

And that was all the encouragement they needed. Wide-eyed apprehension dissolved into happy giggles as a pair of sweet, old mares lipped the apples slices from the girls' palms. After that, the whole group was eager to gather around Jarrett, take turns feeding the horses and listen as he explained the rules of riding.

She'd been more charmed than she wanted to admit, seeing the rugged rancher surrounded by little girls. It was like trying to picture Clint Eastwood in his younger, spaghetti-Western days overseeing a sleepover. Almost impossible to imagine if she hadn't witnessed it for herself.

But she didn't think she could or *should* tell him how he'd impressed her. It was too close to admitting how attracted she was to him. Too close to revealing how much she wished he'd kissed her the other day and how many times that brief moment had crossed her mind.

She'd done her best to deny it and when that failed, to ignore it. She'd purposely worn apparel fitting for working in the stables, kept her hair pulled back in a low ponytail and didn't bother with makeup. It was how she'd looked the first day she arrived and changing now, well, it wasn't as if she could say she'd done it for the horses' benefit.

So she knew she looked about as attractive as a washed-out old dishrag, but she refused to give in. And as much as she wanted to believe it was all about pride, right at that moment, with Jarrett standing just a few feet away as they stepped into the shadowy interior of the stables, she thought maybe it was closer to self-preservation.

If she admitted her attraction to the tough rancher, she'd be that much more likely to give in to it…

Searching her mind for something she *could* say, she responded, "Chloe was really good with them."

"Figured she would be."

Theresa had to smile at the straightforward statement. No overwhelming praise from Jarrett—just an unquestioning confidence in the young girl. And in himself. He was the kind of man who made a decision and lived with it—no second thoughts.

And no second chances?

Memories of the past jabbed at her, forcing their way into the present, into this moment. Even before the accident, Michael had a reserve, a caution she'd always attributed to being a father raising a young daughter single-handedly. But since their split, she'd had time to recognize that shell may well have been a part of his character—an impenetrable wall she would have spent years banging her head against if not for the car crash.

As much as Theresa wanted to believe Michael and Jarrett were as different inside as they were outwardly, she wasn't so certain. Surely, she'd learned her lesson when it came to keeping her distance from the strong, silent type.

Judging by the leap in her pulse when she stopped to face Jarrett, it was a lesson she was in danger of failing a second time. "You figured, huh?"

Theresa tried to inject a teasing note into her voice, but the words came out huskier than she'd intended. With Jarrett standing close enough for her to feel the heat from his body, close enough for her to breathe in the woodsy, masculine scent of him, close enough that she had to tip her head back ever so slightly to see the heat in his green-gold eyes, she was lucky to get the words past the sudden dryness in her throat at all.

"Yep. That's what I figured." His gaze dropped to her lips, and Theresa's breath caught just as it had a few days before when they stood in almost this same spot and she'd wondered what it would be like if he kissed her.

This time she barely had a chance to wonder, barely had a chance to react, when he ducked his head and stole a quick kiss. Her surprised gasp was still stuck in her throat as he was already pulling away, her body swaying toward his, seeking out more of what that brief kiss promised.

"Just like I figured you'd taste like apples." Jarrett's voice was as rough as the roads leading to the cabin, adding another dimension to the words as the sound scraped against raw nerve endings. "A little tart, but mostly sweet. Turns out I was right about that, too."

Chapter Six

"So…" Debbie Mattson's blue eyes gleamed as she leaned forward across the small table. "Tell us what it's like living with Jarrett Deeks."

"I'm staying in one of his cabins, Debbie," Theresa said, even as she hoped the bar's dim lighting would hide the heat rising in her cheeks. "It's not like I've moved in with the guy."

"Close enough." The blonde baker lifted her shoulders in a shrug. "You're there, he's there…"

"Yes, I'm there—in my cabin—and I don't even know where Jarrett sleeps." Although it wouldn't have totally surprised her to discover he had a cot somewhere in the stables. Unless he was out on a trail ride, he didn't ever seem to be anywhere else.

Darcy clicked her tongue, hiding a smile as she shot Kara and Sophia a knowing glance. "And don't you wish you did?"

"Okay, stop or you're going to make me regret coming out tonight!"

Tonight, as it turned out, was Debbie's bachelorette party. With the wedding a week away, her future sisters-in-law, Darcy, Kara and Sophia, were taking the bride-to-be out for her last night on the town as a free woman. Debbie had chosen a restaurant in nearby Redfield, a place where she'd attended a singles' event a few months ago. She'd been looking to meet a handsome stranger to sweep her off her feet—but the real magic of that night had happened when she ran into Drew and started to fall for her good friend.

Theresa had been happy to join them for the party. She'd gotten to know Darcy and Kara when she'd visited in the days before their weddings and had hung out with Debbie years ago when she'd spent summer vacations with her relatives. She'd practically jumped at the chance to escape the quiet cabin and enjoy a girls' night out, but she was beginning to wonder if going to The High Tide was such a good idea. The restaurant had a touristy vibe with fishing nets, wooden oars and large, mounted fish dangling from the walls as part of the decor. The place was known for its seafood, but Theresa had the feeling her cousin and her friends were more interested in grilling *her*.

"You have to excuse them." The most reserved of the group, Kara, explained. "Jarrett Deeks has become something of a mystery around here, and everyone's dying to get the scoop on him."

"And with you living out there," Debbie reiterated, "it only makes sense that you dish away."

"I'm not scooping or dishing—" or kissing "—anyone." Not that anyone had mentioned kissing—that simply seemed to be where her thoughts went more often than not since the kiss early that morning.

If you could call it a kiss. Jarrett had barely given her the chance to respond, sauntering off while she stared after him, her lips still tingling from the electric spark. He'd caught her totally off guard. Next time she'd— Wait, she didn't *want* a next time. She was keeping her distance, remember?

"I picked the cabins because I wanted a place that would offer some peace and quiet," she insisted. "I'm not looking for anything else."

The group's attention turned to the waiter as he arrived with their drinks followed quickly by the mouthwatering combo platter he placed in the center of the table. Though the appetizers—coconut shrimp, calamari rings and potato skins—were the high-fat, high-calorie foods Theresa normally avoided, she'd quickly agreed to share the mix of bar food. The bite-size selections were easy to eat one-handed, allowing her to keep her left arm tucked beneath the table and sparing her—and her friends—the painful embarrassment of watching her struggle to cut up an entrée with a knife and fork.

After making a toast to the bride's and groom's happiness, they divvied up the food, and at the first bite of salty-bacon-and-cheese-sprinkled potato skins, Theresa sighed. Why was it some of the things that were so bad tasted so good?

As delicious as the food was, it didn't keep Debbie distracted for long. "You told us you've been helping out at the stables," she said, pointing a fried shrimp in Theresa's direction. "You and Jarrett must have talked about something."

"He's not exactly an open-up-and-share kind of guy."

All the more reason for her to keep her distance. If she was interested in a guy, she wanted him to be the type to be open with his thoughts and feelings. She didn't want to have to fight to drag out every little bit of emotion, to battle to gain his trust only to lose it in the end, as she had with Michael, knowing she'd never really had it in the first place.

And even if Jarrett didn't have emotional roadblocks set up all around, it was ridiculous to even think in terms of a relationship when she'd be going home in just over three weeks. She wasn't about to start something when the end was already clearly in sight. What would be the point?

Thoughts of what it would be like if Jarrett *really* kissed her teased Theresa's imagination. Three weeks might not be all that long, but it left plenty of time for kissing…and maybe even more if she had the courage to go for it.

With a quick shake of her head, she reached for her glass of water. What was she thinking? That she was going to have some kind of vacation fling with Jarrett Deeks? She'd never had any kind of fling and to even contemplate having one now when her life was in such shambles… Crazy. That's all there was to it.

She was not a fling kind of woman. She'd always taken relationships and intimacy seriously. She and Michael had dated for several months before they slept together and by then, she'd fully expected to marry him someday—and look how that had turned out. All that time planning, all those years of dating, all her certainty in what their future would hold, shattered and broken in one split second.

Maybe living for the day wasn't so crazy. Maybe the real insanity was planning for a future that might never come…

"I know a little bit about his past," Sophia chimed in almost reluctantly as she wiped her crumb-coated fingers on a napkin. "Just what I could find online."

"Oh, good grief!" Kara protested, setting her glass of

white wine back on the table with a soft clink. "Did you *investigate* him?"

"Sophia Cameron, Mrs. PI," Darcy joked.

Sophia raised her hands in an innocent gesture. "I did not investigate him, and I didn't do anything other than find what's public record on the internet."

"But why would you even bother?" Theresa asked.

"Well…" Her cousin shot a glance at her soon-to-be sister-in-law. "There was a time when Darcy and I thought Jarrett might be the right guy for Debbie, and I wanted to find out more about him."

"Oh." Pinpricks of envy stabbed Theresa as she glanced over at the outgoing and curvaceous blonde. "So you and Jarrett—"

After swallowing a sip of her margarita, Debbie shook her head. "Never even went on a date. You don't have to worry. Your cousin pretty much tried to set me up with every single guy in town."

"Not every guy," Sophia protested.

"Not with Drew," Darcy teased as she popped a calamari ring into her mouth. Sophia had been somewhat relentless in trying to set her friend up, not knowing Debbie and her brother were secretly dating.

"I'm not worried," Theresa argued, turning the conversation back toward Debbie's comment. "And I'm not interested in whatever you found online."

"I am!" Debbie and Darcy said in unison.

Theresa opened her mouth to protest but knew it would do no good. The other women would override her unless she was willing to explain how she felt. How she wanted Jarrett to be the one to open up to her.

She felt as if she was cheating. She wanted to earn the silent, solitary rancher's trust. If Jarrett chose to tell her about his past, it would mean…well, a lot more than hearing from Sophia whatever she'd discovered on the internet.

"It's not much," her cousin confessed with an apologetic glance Theresa's way, almost as if Sophia knew what she was thinking. "And since I don't know anything about the rodeo, I'm not sure I even understood all I read. I do know that he was a bull rider, and a good one, too. He was pretty popular."

"Popular?" Kara questioned.

"He had some big-name endorsements before he got hurt."

"What happened?" Drawn into the conversation despite her best attempts to stay out of it, Theresa's heart thudded in her chest at the thought of Jarrett suffering an injury. Instant empathy pulled at her and not, she feared, in a professional nurse-patient capacity.

"He was thrown from a bull." The other women made sympathetic noises, but Sophia shook her head. "That wasn't the worst part. Evidently, getting thrown is a normal part of riding. But when he hit the ground, he couldn't get out of the way in time, and the bull landed on him."

Theresa might not know bulls, but she'd ridden horses long enough to imagine the damage an animal of that size could cause. Broken bones, torn muscles, internal bleeding—not so different from the devastation of a car accident. "How badly was he hurt?"

"I don't know. There were all kinds of stories about his injuries—everything from how he'd only gotten banged up to rumors that he'd never ride again."

"So that was the end of his career?" Theresa couldn't help thinking about the day at the stables when Jarrett had talked about Duke and how the animal had found new life and a new purpose. She'd been so sure he'd been talking about *her*, telling her she would find work in something other than the career she loved. And she'd snapped at him, certain that he didn't have any idea what it was like to have his whole world pulled out from beneath him.

"You'd think so, right? I mean, who would even consider getting on the back of a bull after that, but he did. He competed in a few more rodeos before hanging up his spurs and moving here about a year ago."

"That's it?" Darcy asked, disbelief and disappointment pulling at her eyebrows as she sank back against the padded booth. "What about his personal life? Ex-girlfriends, ex-wives, anything?"

"No ex-wives that I could find and no real mention of family."

He had a half sister, Theresa knew that much, but she wasn't about to share. And Sophia's internet search had left her with more questions than answers.

"Well, at least we know he's single," Darcy surmised as if that was the most important piece of information she'd gleaned from Sophia's research, "so there's no reason for you not to go after him."

"No reason other than that I'm only here for another three weeks."

"That's plenty of time! Give us married and soon-to-be-married women a thrill by letting us live vicariously through your whirlwind romance."

"Darcy!"

The other woman laughed at Theresa's embarrassed protest. "What can a little fantasizing hurt?"

"That's what I thought, too," Debbie added, "until Drew overheard me at *your* bachelorette party."

"And look how that turned out!" Darcy offered a smug smile as if taking credit for the love match. "Just goes to show what can happen if you open your mind to the possibility."

* * *

The lights were on in the small rental office, Theresa noticed as she drove by. Or make that light—a solitary glow shone out from a front window, seeming to speak more of isolation than welcome. It was late, past midnight, and she wondered if that was the only opportunity Jarrett had to handle mundane tasks like paperwork. During the day, the horses and the stables required his attention. In the short time she'd been at the ranch, she didn't think she'd seen him slow down or take a break for more time than it took to drain a bottle of water.

Of course, he was a grown man. Certainly, he was capable of taking care of himself and didn't need her looking out for him. But knowing that didn't stop Theresa from slowing the car and parking in front of the small cabin.

She'd just go in and say good-night. Maybe ask what was on schedule for the morning and see if it was something she and Chloe could handle. It would be no different than a dozen or so conversations they'd had over the past few days. Just because it was after midnight and she felt jazzed from a second wind that came from staying up too late, laughing and hanging out with her friends, that didn't mean anything would happen between her and Jarrett.

She'd jumped to the wrong conclusion that first day at the barn. She'd thought for sure Jarrett had been making comparisons about her life, about how she should move on from her career as an ER nurse, when perhaps he'd been talking about his own experience. Either way, he had a better idea of how she was feeling than…well, just about anyone. Her family could sympathize. They could offer their love and support, but they couldn't understand the pain and loss of having such a big part of her life ripped away.

Jarrett would.

And yet—he seemed so at home on the ranch, working with the horses. He fit into this rugged landscape as if he'd been born to it and had never called another place home. But quiet, little Clearville was a world away from the excitement and energy of the rodeo, and she couldn't help wondering how he'd done it. How he'd made the adjustment. How he'd found the strength to start over with something new…

Be open to the possibilities.

Darcy's words echoed in her thoughts, but Theresa dismissed them. That wasn't what she was doing. She wasn't open, and there were no possibilities. But neither of those facts were enough to make her put the car in Drive. Instead, she cut the engine and climbed out into the chilly night.

Jarrett opened the door almost the instant she knocked, making Theresa wonder if he'd heard the car pull up. If he'd been waiting inside while she debated stopping or driving on. Her cheeks heated a bit and then a little more when he asked, "Everything all right?"

Logical question considering midnight wasn't exactly a typical time for social calls. "It's, um, fine. I just came back from town and saw the light on… Kind of late to be working."

"Kind of late for a night on the town."

"Not really," she protested as he opened the door wider for her to step inside.

"By local standards."

"Okay, that's true." Most shops rolled up around seven even on weekends, which had made going into Redfield and The High Tide not just the best choice but about the only one for the bachelorette party. Debbie hadn't seemed to mind as she declared her wild party days over. Not that Theresa believed her. The outgoing, fun-loving woman was bound to keep Drew Pirelli on his toes—married or not.

"So…you must have had a good time to stay out so late."

"Oh, yeah. We…"

Her voice trailed off as she noticed Jarrett's gaze travel from the top of her head down to the tips of her toes. She'd pulled her hair into a low side ponytail—about as fancy as she could manage—and had worn makeup for the first time since she'd arrived.

She'd ditched her jeans and sweatshirts, too, for one of the nicer outfits she'd had the foresight to bring. A tunic-style red sweater that came to midthigh over a pair of black leggings and ankle boots were fancier than typical dress code at the local bar, but she hadn't felt out of place as the other women had also dressed up for the night. And she was glad now that she'd made the effort. Glad that she could have a conversation with the gorgeous rancher without worrying that she had hay in her hair or that she smelled like horses.

"We went out for Debbie's bachelorette party."

Jarrett nodded but didn't comment. He stepped back as she entered the small space, circling around to the desk, where he'd obviously been sitting before she arrived.

An image flashed in her mind. Jarrett working with one of the horses, keeping his distance and giving the animal room to roam without making it feel cornered or threatened. Was that how he saw her then? Theresa swallowed hard. As broken and damaged as one of his mistreated horses?

Maybe she'd been wrong before. Maybe Jarrett did see rescuing her as part of his job description and she'd completely misread the interest in his eyes.

"I should go," she said abruptly, not caring what he would think about her sudden appearance and equally sudden disappearance.

She didn't expect him to stop her, so she was surprised

when his voice reached out, halting her as effectively as a hand against the door. "Running away, Theresa?"

Her back straightened at the accusation, but she didn't turn around. "Away from what?"

"Whatever brought you here in the first place."

His words were laconic and easy, almost as if he didn't care one way or the other whether she walked out, as if he did care what had brought her to his door so late at night. But they were also spoken much closer. She might not have heard him move, but she could feel him over her shoulder. No longer keeping the length of the room between them, but not crowding her, either.

Stay or go... His distance seemed to be telling her. *It's your choice.*

Ever since the accident, so much of her world had been out of her control. The rate of her recuperation, the possibility of her returning to work, her relationship with Michael and her chance to see Natalie and help the little girl with her own recovery. And the harder she tried to cling to the pieces of her life—pieces shattered and broken by the crash—the more they slipped through her hands. She didn't know how much of it she'd ever be able to put back together, not when so much was missing from what had been before.

She took a deep breath, poised between flight and, well, not fight exactly, though she wasn't sure what would happen if she stayed. She started to turn back toward Jarrett when a photo hanging beside the door caught her eye.

A bull rider captured in midride. Or more like midflight as at least two feet of air separated him from the bull. He seemed tethered only by the rope in his hand. By some miracle, his cowboy hat was still on, pulled low over his forehead, shielding his face, but Theresa knew. Looking at the picture, she felt the same breathlessness, the same excitement, the same connection she'd felt watching Jarrett ride Silver. If she closed her eyes, she was sure she'd hear the roar of the crowd, smell the earthy scent of the animals, feel the tremor in the ground as the massive bull came back to the hard-packed dirt on all four hooves.

She reached out, halfway toward tracing a fingertip over Jarrett's picture, before she caught herself, covering the telling motion by straightening the already-square frame.

"How did you do it?" she asked softly. "How did you just…walk away?"

"Didn't. I was carried off on a stretcher," he answered wryly.

"But then you—" Theresa bit her lip but too late to pretend she didn't know what she did. Sighing, she turned to face him. "I heard that you competed again after the injury."

"You heard, huh?"

"Small town." She shrugged. "You've been here long enough to know there aren't many secrets."

Jarrett scowled a little at the thought, but he didn't appear angry that she'd listened to gossip about his life. She was still surprised, though, when he told her, "At the time I thought it was important that I leave on my own terms."

"And now?"

"Now I pretty much think I was a stubborn ass and as lucky as hell that I *could* walk away considering what the doctors told me might happen if I got thrown again." Shadows lingered in his gaze, deep and dark enough to make Theresa wonder about that fall and the extent of his injuries. "Truth is, I went back because I didn't know what else to do. Didn't think there *was* anything else I could do. Rodeo was my life, and if I couldn't ride…" He gave a half shrug that was anything but casual as he brushed off the loss of his career.

"So how did you get here? Owning a ranch and running the rescue?"

"It's all thanks to my dad…and to Duke."

"Your dad and your horse?" Theresa asked hesitantly.

"Yeah. I'd never been one to believe in fate, but without them, I don't know where I'd be right now. Probably still riding in the rodeo despite the risk—assuming it wouldn't have killed or crippled me by now."

Crippled. The word had her instantly thinking of her own injury but also of the mysterious injury that had led to Jarrett's retirement.

"How warm is that sweater?"

The out-of-the-blue question had Theresa blinking. "Um, warm enough, I guess."

"I don't think so." Reaching out, he grabbed a jacket hanging on the other side of the picture. "You're gonna need this."

"I am?"

"Yep."

"Why?"

"Because it's a long story, and I can't tell long stories sitting still." The corner of his mouth kicked up in a half grin, erasing some of the shadowed memories from his handsome face. "Don't suppose I can talk you into that ride?"

Just a few days ago, that same question had filled Theresa with a sense of heartbreak and loss. But in that moment, an answering smile tugged at her lips and she felt… tempted. But she still shook her head, not ready for the ride or—she feared—the man offering it. "Not tonight."

"Then I guess we'll just have to walk," he said as he draped the jacket over her shoulders. Theresa was immediately blanketed by the faint hint of hay and horses and the piney outdoor scent that Theresa would no longer associate with Clearville but instead with the man himself. "But don't think I didn't notice."

"Notice what?"

He leaned in closer as he murmured, "That you didn't say no this time."

Chapter Seven

"Sure you're warm enough?" Jarrett asked as he led the way down a moonlit path. His breath formed a cloud around the words, though he supposed Northern California nights couldn't compete with Midwestern winters.

Theresa shot him a sideways look. "You're the one without a jacket."

Jarrett shrugged, feeling warm enough in the blue-and-white-flannel button-down he'd pulled on over his long-sleeved T-shirt earlier in the evening. Even if he were freezing, he wouldn't have said anything. Not when the sight of Theresa wearing his jacket filled him with a sense of propriety. The feeling was more fitting for a high school jock handing off his letterman jacket than a grown man, but at the end of the night, he'd be tempted to let her hold on to the denim jacket. Wanting her to keep a part of him, even if he knew better than to expect her to give a piece of herself in return.

And that was what this walk was about, after all, wasn't it? Ever since she arrived, she'd been hanging tough. Telling her relatives and everyone who asked that she was just fine. She'd shown up every day at the stables, even though at times he knew it was a struggle for her. She hid it well, shifting her weight to her right leg, keeping her left hand tucked into the front pocket of the sweatshirts she wore. But he'd noticed her limping toward the end of the day when she thought he wasn't watching. Sensed her frustration when everyday tasks eluded her, and a brush or bridle slipped from her grasp.

But tonight was the first time he'd seen her lower her guard, the first time the vulnerability and sorrow in her blue gaze threatened to overwhelm her. He wouldn't let that happen. He wasn't going to let her give up, and if talking about his past would help…

He'd meant what he said about needing to be outside. In the fresh air and open spaces where he could still breathe and keep his focus on the good times with his father—how he'd learned to ride at Ray's side as his father worked as a foreman on ranches all over the West. He'd idolized his father as a kid and had had the perfect childhood—at least until he turned seven and his mother left his dad—and took Jarrett with her.

He'd hated living in Atlanta and could only be glad his mother had quickly tired of single motherhood. By the time she reconnected with George Carrington—an old-money, old family friend—she'd been ready to put everything about her past with Ray behind her. Including her son.

He knew it hadn't been easy for Ray to put in long hours on a ranch and still take care of a child. Looking back, Jarrett realized he had probably been on his own more than most kids and given more freedom and more responsibility than he'd known at times how to handle. But Ray had done his best and had always been there for him, always looked out for him even when Jarrett hadn't known it.

"A few years before my injury, my dad passed away. He'd had a stroke and by the time the end came, he was ready to go."

Theresa spoke after a brief silence. "That's supposed to make it easier, but I'm not sure it does."

"I guess you've seen your share of heartbreak working in the ER."

"Enough to know how hard it is to see a loved one suffer." Her voice trembled slightly at the end, and he sensed she wasn't talking about a professional case, but a personal one.

"My dad was the one who pretty much raised me. He'd always been there for me, even though I know times were tough and money was usually tight. That's why it was such a surprise to find out he'd had a life insurance policy."

Sometimes he still couldn't believe it. When he looked around the ranch, at the stables he'd pretty much built with his own hands, at the horses he'd helped to save, Jarrett knew he owed it all to his father. The ranch was as much his father's legacy as it was Jarrett's present and future.

"His death hit me hard." He blurted out the words as if by spitting them out quickly he could skip over the dark memories from the time after his father's stroke and the weeks and months following his father's passing. "I'd always been a little reckless, and after he died, I started taking even more chances—and not just in the arena. I was drinking too much, getting in bar brawls, wound up in jail more than once. Only smart thing I did in those years was that I didn't touch a penny of the life insurance money. I'd seen other guys on the circuit blow through their earnings in a few months without a single thing to show for it. I wanted the money to matter. For everything my dad had sacrificed to make the payments for all those years to really mean something."

"And that's when you were injured," Theresa filled in.

"Yep." He'd long grown used to minimizing the extent of his injuries. But how would that help Theresa see that she could move on from her own? "I'd damaged my spinal column." He had to clear his throat to admit the next part, to force his way past the dark memories. "When I woke up, I was paralyzed from the waist down."

He sensed rather than heard her quick intake of breath. He supposed it was part of her training, minimizing her reaction to hearing or even delivering bad news. She probably thought she should be so stoic and professional when it came to facing her own prognosis—whatever it was.

"The doctors told me I'd be lucky if I ever walked again—forget riding. Forget the rodeo." And after seeing his father trapped in a broken, almost lifeless body, Jarrett had understood more than most people how it could be a fate worse than death.

He felt Theresa's hand on his arm—her skin cold despite his borrowed jacket—and he swore beneath his breath. He wanted to pull away, to retreat from the pity he knew he'd see in her eyes as she murmured, "Oh, Jarrett," but he couldn't. Instead, he stopped walking and took her hand within his own and rubbed some warmth back into those delicate fingers.

And when he met her gaze—the bright blue still vivid even in the faint moonlight—his heart slammed against his chest. Because it wasn't pity he saw shining there.

It was pride.

"It's amazing that you've come so far, to have fully recovered from your injury… I know about the determination and hard work that goes into that kind of rehab."

Again, Jarrett didn't think she was speaking from a professional viewpoint, and he hadn't missed the way she kept her left hand tucked within the pocket of his jacket, even while he still held on to her right. Her soft skin was warmer now, the delicacy of the fine bones somewhat misleading. Theresa was tough. Stronger and more capable than she gave herself credit for. He didn't doubt she'd pushed herself as hard during her rehab as he once had.

"Recovery was tough. Harder and more painful than anything I'd experienced riding bulls. And even when I beat all the odds against me, even when I was stupid enough to go back to competing, I still had to face knowing my life would never be the same. Would never be what I'd imagined. I'd been traveling from rodeo to rodeo, living for the rush of performing in front of screaming crowds for so long, I didn't know how I'd get on without it. But then I found Duke and had the idea for starting the rescue. It's not the road I planned to travel, but it brought me here, and this is home now."

"Be open to the possibilities," Theresa murmured.

"What was that?"

She shook her head as if wishing the words back. "Just something Darcy said tonight."

"Sounds like good advice."

She met his gaze in the moonlight, silent for a heartbeat or two too long. Enough time for Jarrett to sense her willingness to take that advice could end up having a lasting effect on his life… "Maybe it is," she conceded finally. Only then seeming to notice that he still held her hand, she took a step back and drew away.

Feeling the loss, he tucked his hands into his back pockets. Funny that he would feel cold without her touch when he'd been the one trying to warm her hand in the first place. A memory played on the edges of his mind, and he asked, "Do you know the first time I saw you?"

Her eyebrows drew together in a puzzled frown. "Sitting on your office porch a few days ago?"

"Um, no," Jarrett confessed, mentally smacking himself. Way to point out how aware he'd been of her occasional visits when she'd had no reason to make note of him at all. But hell, he'd already stuck his foot in it, so why not kick it around some?

"It was when you came to town last summer for Sophia's wedding. I was in town at the diner when a little girl started having an attack—"

"I remember that. It was one of my niece's friends. She had an asthma attack and didn't have her inhaler with her."

"Everyone else was freaking out—talking about calling 911 and rushing her to the hospital." Even from across the room, he'd seen how the panic going on around the young girl was only making matters worse. "And then you took over."

Theresa had stepped into the middle of the confusion, calming the frantic adults with little more than a word or two before focusing on the little girl. He could still picture the girl's pale face, her eyes wide with fear, as she struggled to breathe, and he could hear Theresa's soothing voice as she encouraged the girl to breathe in through her nose and out through her mouth as if blowing out candles on a birthday cake.

"What you did that day had nothing to do with physical strength. There were half a dozen guys at the diner— myself included—who were physically stronger than you, but that didn't make a lick of difference. Your caring and compassion were what mattered then, and that's what will matter in the future, too."

* * *

Theresa recalled the day Jarrett was talking about—remembering the girl's asthma attack and her babysitter's frantic realization that she'd forgotten to bring along an inhaler. She'd gone to the diner with Sophia, and the two of them were laughing over some of their teenage exploits when she first became aware of the little girl having trouble breathing. Her training had taken over, and she'd rushed to the girl's side.

She remembered all of that, including the familiar satisfaction of helping in a crisis...

Theresa didn't know how many words of encouragement she'd heard in the months since the accident from family and friends and coworkers. She'd done her best to listen, to take heart in what they were saying. To try to believe she *hadn't* lost everything and that her life *would* get better. She'd even reached a point where she could offer the appropriate responses and reassure those around her that she, too, knew she would be okay.

But she'd never truly believed what she was saying because she'd never been completely honest. Not with her concerned friends and family and not with herself. She'd buried the deepest of her fears where she wouldn't have to face them. The last thing she expected was for them all to start spilling out on a moonlight walk with Jarrett Deeks.

"The doctors can't say for sure if the nerve damage in my hand will completely heal. At least not to the point where I could go back to working in the ER. And even if I could, I'm not sure I want to go back. I used to love going to the hospital, but now... It's a demanding job—physically and emotionally—and sometimes the thought of caring for patients..."

You can't even take care of yourself. How do you expect to help anyone else?

Michael's angry voice echoed against the walls of her memory. Upon waking in the hospital, Theresa's only focus had been on his daughter, Natalie. She'd refused to rest until she could see the little girl for herself. Her fellow nurses had bent the rules by wheeling her up to the ICU. All she wanted to do was help, to care for the little girl she'd already started to love as her own.

But she never made it to Natalie's side. Michael had stopped her short, throwing her helplessness into her face and freezing her with his icy fury. And as much as she'd tried to deflect the bitter slice of those words, every time she took a stumbling step, every time her fingers couldn't complete the simplest task, his accusation cut into her again and again.

"I just don't know if I have it in me anymore to be the nurse I once was."

The admission was gut-wrenching. As if she were taking a dull knife and slicing away at her insides. But instead of removing a cancer, she felt as though she were cutting out the best, most meaningful part of herself and throwing it away.

"You do."

He spoke the words with such certainty, as if it were just that easy. Anger washed away the shame, and she opened her mouth to fire off a retort. What did he know about starting over? Easy for him to say things would get better!

Only he did know better than anyone what she was going through, and it hadn't been easy. "I wish— I wish I could believe that."

"Believe it. The day at the diner… You were amazing."

Her small smile trembled around the edges as she pointed out, "*Were* being the key word."

"Caring about people isn't something you do, it's who you are. Tell me the truth, you were about to kick my butt the other day when you thought I wasn't sympathizing enough with Chloe having to give up her horse."

Why did it even surprise her that he'd noticed her reaction when at the time he hadn't seemed to be paying attention to her at all? It seemed to be a talent of his—an extra awareness of where she was and what she was doing—and Theresa didn't know if the idea left her feeling more flustered or flattered...

"I doubt I would have resorted to physical violence, but I was planning to give you a piece of my mind," she admitted with a smile.

"All because you cared that much about a girl you'd just met. No car accident is going to change that. That part of you is just as strong as it was the day in the diner."

"I still can't believe you were there."

Jarrett shrugged, but the look in his gaze was far from casual. "It's a small town."

"I know but..."

How could it be that they'd both been at the small diner and yet she hadn't noticed him? Walking beside him now, so very aware of *everything* about him—from the sound of his breathing, the cadence of his step, the occasional brush of his shoulder against hers—she didn't know how that was possible. With the quiet stillness of the night, her every sense seemed tuned in solely to Jarrett. His voice was the only sound she heard, his scent was the air she breathed, and when his gaze captured hers, she couldn't bring herself to look away.

She'd been wrong before. Jarrett wasn't going to feel sorry for her. He didn't see her as broken, and if there was any comparison between the way he treated her and the way he treated his rescue horses, it was only in the patience he showed, in his willingness to let her take the lead and make the first move.

As first moves went, hers started out as a tentative one. Reaching up to touch his face. But the moment she felt the slight scrape of his whiskered jawline against her finger-tips, her hesitation evaporated, burned away by the sudden rush of need and desire. She whispered his name, the shaky sound lingering in the cool night air along with the white cloud of her breath, but then the sound, the air, the breath, was lost in his kiss.

His fingers—calloused and workman tough—traced over her cheeks, her ears, her neck, before sinking into her hair. He held her lightly as if letting her know it was still her call, but control was an illusion. She was captured by his kiss, caught up in the desire she'd felt from the first moment they met, and she didn't know how she would break free. Not that freedom mattered at the moment, either. Not when there was nowhere else she wanted to be than in his arms.

Heat spread through her veins, building hotter, faster, until she was gasping for air. Her head fell back, and his teeth lightly scored the side of her neck. Shudders racked her body, and her fingers tightened in the soft flannel of his shirt, but she was desperate for the smooth skin and masculine muscle beneath. Skin-to-skin contact with nothing in between…

The intensity of that need startled her. *Scared* her. This wasn't like her. She didn't rush into relationships. And certainly didn't make out with men she'd just met! "Jarrett." This whispered rush of air sounded more like encouragement than protest, but he pulled away. He could already read her so well.

His hazel eyes glittered in the faint moonlight, and only the sound of their combined breathing broke the silence of the night around them. "Looks like I've walked you home," he murmured, and Theresa was surprised to realize her cabin was just around a curve in the gravel path.

So close, and for a split second, she let herself think of what might happen if she invited Jarrett inside. "I'm only here for another few weeks."

She intended the statement as a warning, a reason for them to take a step back, to slow down. But the longing behind the words—and the heat in Jarrett's shadowed gaze that followed her as she walked those last few yards to the cabin alone—only made them seem like a reason to hurry...

Chapter Eight

"You Jarrett Deeks?"

Jarrett glanced over his shoulder at the deep voice behind him. He unclipped the lead from Duke's bridle, turned the horse loose in the corral and swung the gate shut with a reverberating clang before answering, "I'm Deeks."

He'd been honest with Theresa about his past and occasional run-ins with the law. He'd put those days and that recklessness behind him, but he still had a healthy respect for the law as well as an ability to spot a cop.

The guy standing a few feet away definitely had the look. Close-cut dark hair, a relaxed yet ready bearing that screamed either police or military. Though he couldn't see behind the other man's reflective sunglasses, Jarrett had a feeling the other guy was sizing him up. He didn't know for sure that this guy was a cop, but if he was, he was out of his jurisdiction. This was no deputy on the local force.

"I'm looking for one of your guests, Theresa Pirelli. Can you tell me what cabin she's in?"

On a cold day in hell, Jarrett thought.

This wasn't the golden-boy doctor Theresa brought with her on her last visit, but even if Jarrett had recognized him as one of her boyfriends, he wasn't about to make it easy on the guy.

"Sorry." He braced a hand against the top bar of the corral's fence. "Company policy not to give out information on our guests."

"Right, because this place is so five star," the other man murmured.

Jarrett didn't let the sarcasm get to him. Instead, he hid a grin as the other man took an awkward step to avoid a pile of manure Duke had left behind.

City boy, he thought, only to remember that Theresa—despite her gift with horses—was very much a city girl. Which probably made last night's kiss a mistake. Even if it was the best mistake he'd ever made.

Her lips had been cold but sweet and warmed quickly beneath his, adding a hint of spice to the sweet, an addictive combination that left him wanting more.

I'm only here for another few weeks.

A simple-enough statement at face value, but he'd stayed up half the night trying to read between the lines. Theresa would only be in town for a few more weeks, so those few kisses were all they'd share? Or she'd only be in town for a few weeks, so they needed to make the most of the time they had?

For a man known for his patience when it came to the horses he rescued and trained, Jarrett battled the urge to rush, to push. He knew better. That was the fast track to failure. Whatever happened—or didn't happen—between him and Theresa would be up to her. She was the one with a life waiting for her back in the city, and Jarrett wanted her to return without any regrets.

He might not know everything about her life in St. Louis, but he could count on one thing. Theresa wouldn't have kissed him if she'd been involved with anyone. He took a closer look at the man in front of him—the dark hair, the shape of his brow and stubborn set of his jaw—and suddenly saw the resemblance. Not so much between him and Theresa, but of the guy and Drew and Nick. This was a relative; he'd bet on it.

Relaxing a little, he drawled, "I can ring her room if you'd like."

"I'll tell you what I'd like…" The man all but growled only to be interrupted by a female cry.

"Alex! Oh, my gosh, Alex!"

Both men turned to see Theresa approaching. She looked fresh-faced and beautiful with her dark hair caught back in a simple ponytail and wearing the standard jeans and sweatshirt Jarrett had seen her in since she arrived… until last night. Last night, when a ripe-cherry-red sweater and black leggings hugged her curves, when makeup emphasized the mysterious midnight of her eyes and, God help him, made her lips irresistible.

At first her blinding smile and the spark in her brilliant blue eyes were solely for the new arrival. But after that quick second, her gaze cut toward Jarrett. The moment caught and held as his heart thudded in his chest, the rapid beat seeming to count down the limited time they had left.

Only a few weeks…

Theresa greeted Alex with a hug. "I can't believe you're here. When I talked to Mom last week, she didn't know if you'd be able to make it to the wedding."

Alex shrugged. "Things changed and…here I am."

"You're here and— Oh, have you met Jarrett?"

"Not officially," the man said, giving Jarrett the feeling

that he'd just as soon have the *official* meeting take place in an interrogation room somewhere.

"Jarrett, this is my brother Alex."

"Pleasure," her brother said as he shook Jarrett's hand with a grip more suited to arm wrestling than a simple handshake.

But Jarrett had never been one to back down from a challenge, and it would take more than her big brother to keep him away from Theresa.

"I still can't believe you're here," Theresa exclaimed as she looked her brother over. His undercover work took him away for months at a time, and the whole family worried during those long stretches when he was out of touch. "Are Mom and Dad—"

"Coming in right before the wedding. They know how busy Aunt Vanessa and Uncle Vince are going to be leading up to the big day. They don't want to add to the pressure of them having to worry about entertaining family."

"And Max and Tony?" she asked of their brothers, figuring she already knew the answer.

"Max, yeah." Alex didn't even mention their black-sheep brother's name. Tony avoided just about all family events like the plague. Throw in that the wedding was in Clearville and no way would he step foot in the small town. "But I wanted to come in a few days before the wedding since I missed the last two."

Alex had been on assignment when both Nick and Sam got married, and though the family was accustomed to his absences, Theresa couldn't help wondering if her brother wouldn't someday look back with regret at all he'd missed. Still, she said what everyone in the family always did. "I'm just glad you're here now."

"You didn't seem so thrilled a few minutes ago."

"What? You mean when you were acting all macho?" She hadn't missed the death-grip handshake he'd exchanged with Jarrett. She would have been more embarrassed by his behavior if Jarrett hadn't taken the challenge head-on. Instead of wanting to separate them, she'd been tempted to crack both their heads together.

"Give me a break—I wasn't acting."

Theresa couldn't help laughing at the arrogant look Alex shot her. Her brother was a tough guy, no doubt about it. When he grew his hair out for undercover assignments, he looked every bit the hardened criminal. And when his hair was cut short, as it was now, he was very much the hardened cop. But either way, he was still her big brother and, at least from her point of view, more pain in the ass than badass.

"You were being a jerk."

"I was looking out for my little sister."

"Who isn't little anymore and doesn't need your protection."

"Hey, if you'd listened to me about Michael—"

"Seriously? You're going there?" She stopped abruptly, her mild annoyance at his attitude sharpening toward anger.

Alex turned to face her, a muscle working in his jaw as he held back everything she knew he wanted to say. *If you'd listened to me then...*

Alex and the rest of her family had never totally approved of Michael. Oh, sure, as a handsome, successful surgeon, he had all the credentials of an amazing catch. But he'd never warmed to her loud and loving family. She'd tried to explain that Michael was simply overwhelmed by the boisterous Pirelli clan, but her brothers especially had seen the doctor as cold and unbending.

That they'd been right didn't make their *I told you sos* any easier to swallow.

And proving he was a better man than her ex, Alex had the grace to apologize. Exhaling a breath, he said, "You're right. The past is the past, and I shouldn't have brought it up."

"I appreciate that."

"I'm sure you'll appreciate this even more," he said with a grimace that pretty much guaranteed she'd feel the opposite. "Mom wanted me to remind you that you need to get going on the paperwork if you plan to start school during the next session."

"I've told her I'm not interested, but she still keeps pushing." Theresa sighed, her frustration tempered by the knowledge of how much her mother loved her.

"It would help if you'd push back."

"How? I've already told her—"

He shot her a knowing look. "Actions speak louder than words, sis. You need to get back to the ER."

"I haven't been cleared to return to work." The words were the truth, but they left the bitter aftertaste of a lie in her mouth. Physical limitations and the need for medical clearance weren't the only reasons she hadn't gone back to the hospital.

Alex waved aside her protest, and Theresa knew it would take more than doctor's orders to keep him away from his job. "Show them you're ready. Go back to the hospital and prove it. You're not the desk-job type. You're too much like me, needing to be part of the action."

Theresa wished she could believe she was as brave and fearless as her brother. That she'd be able to pick up the pieces of her life and her career as if the car accident had never happened.

Caring about people isn't something you do, it's who you are.

Jarrett's voice was still whispering through her thoughts when her brother demanded, "So what's with the cowboy?"

Squelching an automatic and guilty-sounding denial, she shrugged as she said, "He owns the place and runs a horse rescue, as well. I've been helping out at the stables."

"Let me rephrase the question," Alex said, sounding more like a lawyer than a cop. "What's with you and the cowboy?"

"He owns the place. I'm helping out at the stables," Theresa repeated, refusing to give in to the blush inching up her cheeks or to look away from her brother's penetrating gaze. She wasn't a kid anymore, and she certainly didn't need her big brother warning off any guys who might be interested in her.

Alex gave a short laugh. "Yeah, right. Try again."

"Is this the part where I should plead the fifth?"

"You're not under oath."

"Call for a lawyer?"

"I'm not interrogating you."

"Really?"

Alex shot her a look, but she could see the smile he was trying to hide. But his expression sobered as he said, "I'm worried about you."

"I just need some time to figure out my next step."

"Taking time is a good idea, but your next step is about two thousand miles away."

Back to St. Louis... Back to the ER...

"Any moves you make out here are only going to be in the wrong direction."

Theresa shook her head at the warning in his voice. "Alex, you don't know what you're talking about. I've only known Jarrett for a few days."

But he'd known her for much longer… Or at least he'd been aware of her enough to recall the day at the diner and an incident that had taken place months ago. It was pointless to play what-if games, but she hadn't been able to stop herself from wondering what might have happened if she, too, had noticed Jarrett that day…

Nothing, of course, because she'd been engaged at the time and in love with the man she planned to marry.

But a part of her still wondered…still wished she'd had the chance to meet Jarrett when she was at her best. When she'd felt strong, confident, ready and willing to take on the world. That was the woman she wanted Jarrett to see when he looked at her now. She hated feeling so uncertain, so vulnerable.

And yet, she hadn't felt that way at all when she'd kissed him, had she? Or as if he was making any comparisons to the woman she'd been before.

No, that kiss had been very much in the moment, very much a part of the here and now without looking at the "what might have been" of the distant past and instead focusing very much on the "what could be" in the very near future.

"It doesn't matter how long you've known each other," Alex argued. "I know when a guy is interested."

"Well, you are very attractive," she pointed out, years of pulling his chain making it so easy for her to find a firm handle, even if her thoughts were still on Jarrett's kiss and the moves Alex didn't want her making. "But I honestly don't think you're Jarrett's type."

"I meant, I can tell when a guy is interested in a woman," he gritted out.

Careful to keep the smile from blooming across her face, Theresa asked, "And what did Jarrett do to make you think he's interested in me?"

"It was the way he got all…protective. Wouldn't tell me what cabin you were staying in—"

"So, you'd like it better if he gave out information to total strangers?"

"I'm no stranger."

"Did Jarrett know that?"

"No, but—"

"So in other words, he was just doing his job, and you are the one getting all bent out of shape and overprotective?"

Her brother met her arched gaze for a moment before he shook his head. "I think I need that lawyer."

This time Theresa didn't bother hiding her smile.

Her brother's early and unexpected arrival was a cause for celebration. Her aunt and uncle had invited everyone over the next day for dinner despite Alex's protest that they had enough on their plates already with planning for the wedding.

Aunt Vanessa waved aside his concern. "The wedding is still three days away," she said as she loaded down the large table with a juicy pot roast, garlic mashed potatoes and steamed vegetables, "and we all still need to eat."

"Speak for yourself," Debbie said wryly, making everyone laugh. Like most brides, Debbie was trying to lose a few pounds prior to the big day. But when Drew leaned close and whispered something to his fiancée, bringing a blush to her cheeks, it was clear he thought the woman he loved was already perfect.

The chance to spend time with her extended family had been wonderful, but Theresa exhaled a sigh of relief as she drove back to the peace of Jarrett's property. It was amazing how each of her cousins had found their soul mates within the past year, and she couldn't help feeling a bit overwhelmed and, well, *lonely* in the face of all those loving couples.

Oh, she hadn't been the only single one there. Alex was a die-hard bachelor. *Die-hard...* Not the best description she could use, knowing part of her brother's determination to stay single was because of the risky work he did and his concern about leaving a wife and child behind.

But if Alex felt the least bit out of place as the other single member in the group, he hadn't let it show. He'd joked around with Nick, Drew and Sam and flirted shamelessly with his cousins' significant others. And at the end of the evening, he'd stopped Theresa at her car and tried to talk her into staying in town.

"The wedding reception's at The Hillcrest," he said, naming the Victorian mansion that had been converted into an elegant hotel. "It makes more sense to stay there."

"Um, and it costs a lot more *cents*, too," she pointed out. "I'm not just staying for a few days like you are. I'm here another few weeks."

The phrase echoed in her thoughts, but Theresa no longer knew the meaning behind the words. Was it a protest... or a promise?

Alex scowled at her, and she had to force herself to steadily meet his gaze. Her brother couldn't know the temptation Jarrett Deeks posed or the possibilities that teased her thoughts and dreams of how the two of them might spend those weeks.

"You need to get back home, Theresa. Running from your problems only delays solving them. Staying here—this thing with the cowboy—"

"There is no *thing* with the cowboy," she protested. Uselessly, it turned out, as Alex talked right over her denial.

"It's just a distraction."

"Alex, you don't know—"

"You think I haven't done the same damn thing? After a tough case or an undercover assignment I thought would never end, do you think I haven't tried losing myself one way or another? It doesn't work, Theresa," he said flatly. "Your problems will still be there waiting for you if they aren't already dogging your heels."

Theresa still felt the ache in her chest at her brother's words. For Alex and the darkness he'd witnessed, and for herself, knowing that he was probably right. But she still hadn't given in to moving to the hotel.

She was driving past the stables on her way to the rental cabin when she spotted Chloe racing toward her. In the faint moonlight, Theresa couldn't clearly see the girl's features, but her wildly waving arms were enough to make Theresa slam on the brakes.

She was already climbing from the car by the time Chloe reached her. Worry gave way to relief as the girl dropped her arms to her sides. "Oh, thank goodness you're back! There's been an accident."

Accident… Theresa could barely swallow around the lump in her throat. Oh, God, what had happened? "Is it… Jarrett?"

Her panicked gaze cut toward the corrals, but the horses were calmly milling about. No sign of distress, but also no sign of Jarrett. What had he told her? That another fall could leave him paralyzed?

Her worst fears were confirmed as Chloe nodded, her blond ponytail bobbing, as she grabbed Theresa. "You have to help him."

Chapter Nine

An icy chill crept around Theresa's heart at Chloe's words. Her focus dropped to their linked hands. Chloe's fingers tightly grasping her palm while her own barely closed. Theresa didn't know how long she would have stood there, frozen like the nerves in her hand, if not for the teen pulling her into action. "Come on."

Theresa stumbled after the girl toward the stables. Inside, she again registered the peacefulness, the normality of the horses in their stalls. A few large heads peeked out at their arrival, blinking curiously, while another greeted them with the pawing stomp of a hoof and a gusty blow of air, but there was nothing to reveal what had happened.

"Chloe—"

"He's in here." The girl led the way down a narrow hall past the tack room. A light glowed in what Theresa realized was a small bathroom. She could see Jarrett standing at the sink, his broad shoulders nearly filling the narrow doorway. She took a quick inventory of all she could see. From the flannel-clad shoulders down to his narrow waist, lean hips and long legs, nothing but 100 percent healthy male, and her fear started to fade as the ice around her heart melted beneath a growing warmth.

He looked up as they approached, and Theresa met his gaze in the small mirror. He greeted her with a scowl and ducked his head. "Dammit, Chloe, I told you I'm fine."

As Theresa drew closer, she caught sight of a bloody rag on the vanity and realized why he was standing over the sink.

"You need to look at his hand. It's all…," Chloe swallowed, the color draining from her face.

"Chloe!" The girl started at Theresa's sharp voice. Once she was sure the teen wasn't going to faint, she gently said, "Thank you for coming to get me. You did a good job, no matter what he says." Ignoring the snort coming from the bathroom, she guided Chloe back down the hall and reassured her that everything would be fine.

"Are you sure I shouldn't stay?"

Judging by the paleness of her face earlier, if Chloe stayed, Theresa would likely have two patients on her hands. "I'm sure. Go on home, and I'll see you tomorrow."

The girl promised to return right after school the next day and then surprised Theresa with an impromptu hug. "Thanks for taking care of him. He needs you, you know."

Trying not to read more into the words than the girl had intended, Theresa wished her good-night and then hurried back to the bathroom. The tiny space that consisted of a vanity sink and toilet barely had room for one person, let alone two, but she squeezed by Jarrett to stand at his side and examine his injury. Or to try, as he already had his hand wrapped in a towel.

"Really?" she asked.

Heaving a disgruntled sigh, he unwrapped the towel. As she got her first good look, Theresa could understand why Chloe had reacted the way she had. The length of Jarrett's palm was sliced open. The jagged gash was deepest at the base of his thumb and, while certainly not life threatening or even bleeding as much as Theresa would have expected, it had to hurt. The wound would also leave a scar to go along with half a dozen others she could see on his hand and muscular forearm alone. Some faded to white, others still slightly pink, each one a testimony of hard work.

Michael had always been so careful with his hands, and as a surgeon, rightfully so. Jarrett's hands were far more masculine—rugged and rough—and yet Theresa couldn't help remembering how gentle they'd been when he'd traced her features with his fingertips as they'd kissed.

Forcing herself to focus on his injury, she asked, "What happened?"

"There are still some old fences on the property, marking boundaries between neighboring farms back from who knows when. I've been tearing them down whenever I have some free time. I was piling the wood in the back of my pickup when the stack started to fall. I reached out to catch the boards and caught a nail instead."

"You need stitches."

"I have a first-aid kit. It'll be fine."

"A bandage is not going to fix this," she warned, even as she reached for the box sitting on the toilet lid. Jarrett's first-aid kit was packed with far more than bandages, which made her wonder if it was left over from his days in the rodeo or if running the ranch posed more hazards than she imagined.

"Use the superglue."

Sure enough, a bottle of medical adhesive rested in the top section of the kit, making her wonder how many times he'd patched himself up over the years. "This won't hold as well, especially considering how the skin's going to pull every time you open your hand."

"It'll do." Sheer stubbornness stared back at her, and Theresa knew she'd never talk him into a trip to the clinic in town.

"Fine. At least tell me your tetanus shot is up-to-date."

"Yeah, it's not the first time I've taken on rusty metal and lost." He shrugged off the injury, but Theresa could see he'd taken on more than a dilapidated fence. Shadows darkened his eyes, and the evening scruff on his jaw only added to his worn appearance.

Thinking of his old injury, she said, "You're pushing yourself too hard."

"I'm fine." Determination hardened his jaw, and Theresa knew he'd be making the same claim if he'd cut his hand clean off.

As Jarrett picked up the rag and tossed it aside, she could see that the blood was dried and realized why the cut wasn't still bleeding. "I saw your truck earlier."

"What?"

"When I left to go to dinner, you were already back," she accused as she reached for a small bottle of peroxide.

"So?"

"So, why didn't you come to me right away?"

"Because it's not your job."

Theresa paused for a split second, hurt more than she wanted to admit that he hadn't asked for her help. "Technically, it still is."

Jarrett swore beneath his breath. "I meant that you're not here as a nurse. You're here as a guest. You shouldn't have to take care of me."

The gruffness in his voice rubbed away her annoyance. How long had it been, she wondered, since he'd let anyone take care of him? Since he'd allowed anyone close enough to care *for* him? The walls he put up were good, solid reasons for her to stay back, but the faint cracks—the weaknesses in those walls—kept drawing her closer, tempting her to reach inside.

As she reached for his hand, the other reason why she had a hard time staying away became almost impossible to ignore. Instant awareness streaked through her at the simple touch of taking his hand within her own. The brush of his knuckles against her palm had goose bumps rising to attention all along her arm and chest. Standing so close, she couldn't help but breathe in his scent—a hint of soap and leather combined with honest, hardworking man—and a tiny shiver quaked through her entire body.

It was ridiculous! How many men—patients—had she treated over the years? And none of them affected her the way Jarrett did. Of course, she'd never kissed any of her patients or considered a vacation fling with any of them, either.

Could she really do it? Make love without being in love? Theresa didn't know if she'd be able to. Didn't know if she wanted to be the type of woman who could… And if she did allow herself to be that open, that vulnerable, how hard would it be to walk away in the end?

"This is going to hurt," she said, wondering if she'd intended the words as a warning for Jarrett or for herself.

He hissed out a breath as she poured the peroxide over his hand. "That stuff I said about how caring and compassionate you are? I take it all back."

"Not all my patients are sweet little girls having asthma attacks. Some are hardheaded ranchers too stubborn and proud for their own good."

The sharp smell of disinfectant filled the small space, wiping away her earlier feminine reactions as her training took over. She stumbled slightly as she tried to rip open the packages of sterile gauze, the fingers of her left hand refusing to close tightly enough for her to get a grip with her right. Undaunted, she caught the end of the package between her teeth and ripped the top away. She sensed Jarrett's body tightening, but couldn't figure out why when she had yet to use the gauze to dry the cut. The butterfly bandages were another challenge, but she managed to adhere the tiny strips on either side of the ragged skin, hoping they'd help hold the cut closed as it healed.

Only after she'd cleaned up the wrappings from the gauze and bandages, dropping them in the small wastebasket tucked behind the toilet, did Theresa dare meet Jarrett's gaze. She'd been aware—too aware—of his gaze focused on her face the whole time she worked. If she'd looked up any earlier, she feared she would have lost all sense of professionalism and gone right ahead and tried to kiss it and make it better, and she didn't think she would have just stopped at his hand.

"Damn," he murmured quietly. "I knew you were something that day in the diner, but that was nothing."

Theresa felt her face heat at the look in his eyes—a mix of admiration and desire—but shook her head. "*This* was nothing," she insisted as she led the way back down the narrow hallway and to his office in the stables.

If the cut had been the slightest bit deeper, her efforts would have been useless. He would have needed stitches, and she didn't fool herself into thinking she could manage sutures one-handed.

"I know what you're thinking, but one bandage doesn't prove that I can still do my job." Despite her warning, Jarrett's smile was still far too smug. "And please do not tell me you practically impaled your hand on a rusty old nail just to make a point—no pun intended."

He gave a quick bark of laughter. "Well, as much as I'd like you to think I was being that noble, truth is I was just that clumsy and careless."

"I don't think you're clumsy…or careless."

"Yeah, well, I'm not so noble, either." Catching her wrist with his uninjured hand, he pulled her closer. "If I was, I probably wouldn't be telling you how much I want you right now."

"You don't."

A dark eyebrow winged upward in challenge. "Pretty sure I do."

Theresa ducked her head to try to escape the heat in his gaze. "Stop looking at me like that."

"Like what? Like I think that you're amazing? Like how all I could think about for the past fifteen minutes was how I wished you were touching more than my hand?"

"I dumped peroxide on your hand."

"Well, maybe I don't want to repeat that part but the rest…"

"You're crazy, you know that, right? And you're wrong about me. I'm not amazing. I'm not this remarkable person you think I am! I'm—I'm a mess. After the accident, after Michael…"

Theresa took a step back and freed herself from his grasp to wrap her left arm around her waist as she blurted out, "We were engaged. Did you know that?"

"Yeah."

They had planned a June wedding, so traditional, so perfect… "I loved him, and I really thought he loved me. But after the accident— I wanted to fix things so badly, to help, but I was stuck in that hospital bed, and there wasn't a single thing I could do—"

Theresa didn't remember much from the actual car crash, but she did have one brief, vivid memory of the seat belt snapping tight against her chest at the moment of impact. So tight it had robbed her of breath as it had seemed to strike a solid blow against her heart. When Michael had stood over her in the hospital, when he'd hurled his accusations at her, she'd felt that same blow, same breathlessness, same heartbreak again.

"The SOB broke up with you when you were in the hospital?" Jarrett broke in. He swore beneath his breath. "He doesn't deserve you, Theresa. Not another second of your time."

Certainty hardened the stubborn line of his jaw, but a flash in his eyes hinted at something more. A reflection of the pain she'd felt at Michael's desertion—almost as if he knew what she'd gone through.

But there was something he couldn't know. "I wasn't the only one in the car, Jarrett. Michael's daughter, Natalie, was with me. He—he blamed me for the accident." Just speaking the words, making that admission, Theresa heard the guilt in her voice. If only Natalie hadn't gone with her that day…

Stepping closer, Jarrett pulled her into his arms, and this time, Theresa couldn't find the will to pull away. The comfort and security promised to block out the rest of the world until nothing remained but the warmth of his embrace and the beat of his heart.

"Is she all right?"

"She was in a coma for the first few weeks."

As devastating as the accident had been for Theresa, Natalie was lucky to have survived. When she awoke, the doctors had cautioned them of the long road to recovery as the little girl relearned some of the most basic motor skills.

My daughter is lying in a hospital bed, and it's all your fault!

The accident hadn't been her fault. Logically, she knew

that and thought perhaps even Michael did, too, though feelings of pain and fear and, yes, guilt made it too hard to see clearly. Alex had made a point of talking with the police officers who'd arrived on the scene and told Theresa again and again there was nothing she could have done to prevent the accident.

But Theresa still couldn't shake the overwhelming sense of responsibility. Because while the accident might not have been her fault, she was certainly the reason Natalie had been in the car with her. She'd wanted—had fought for—the opportunity to get to know the girl who would soon be her stepdaughter.

"Michael was so protective of Natalie, so dedicated to his role as a single father. At first, it was one of the reasons I was attracted to him. Family has always been such a big part of my life, too. But after a while, as much as I admired his almost single-minded devotion to his daughter, it started to be a stumbling block. How could we be a family if I was a third wheel when it came to his daughter? So I pushed…"

As she'd done in far too many aspects of their relationship, she feared. She'd convinced Michael that shopping for a flower girl dress was a "girls only" outing. Her heart had nearly burst from her chest when Natalie seriously stated, "No boys allowed, Daddy!"

And Michael had reluctantly agreed to let his baby girl go with Theresa.

If she hadn't pushed so hard— If she hadn't practically backed Michael into a corner— If she'd just bought a few stupid dresses and had Natalie try them on at the house—

If…if…if… The endless wishing didn't change reality one iota, and yet they cemented the weight of guilt so solidly in her heart, Theresa sometimes woke in the middle of the night, panicked and sweating, unable to breathe.

"We were on our way back from the bridal shop. Natalie was so excited about the flower girl dress we found for her. She called it a princess dress and asked if she could wear a tiara. I told her we could see about having the florist weave some teacup roses and baby's breath into her hair instead. She'd laughed and said baby's breath was a funny name, and then the light turned green…"

Theresa shook her head, as if trying to shake the memory away. "The other driver was in an SUV. A mother with three kids in the backseat. She'd turned around, taking her eyes off the road, and didn't realize the light had changed."

"It was an accident," Jarrett concluded, his hand strong and firm on her shoulder blade. "You said Natalie *was* in a coma," he prompted, and a tiniest bit of that pressure eased as she thought of Natalie's improvement.

"She's made some great progress. Better than anyone expected. I just— I wish I could have been there for her. Wish I could have helped take care of her." She gave a short laugh. "Selfish of me, isn't it? After all, if Natalie gets better then maybe I won't feel so responsible, right?"

"There's nothing selfish about it or about you. If Michael had been driving the car that day, would you feel any differently? Would you be any less concerned about Natalie's recovery?"

"No…"

"No. Of course not. You've dedicated your life to helping people. I don't have a single doubt that you would have done anything to protect Natalie. Your jerk of an ex sure as hell should have known that much about you, too."

Instead, he'd turned his back on her when she'd needed him most, a pain Jarrett was all too familiar with, and shaken her confidence—not just personally but professionally as well, by making her doubt her own abilities.

It was enough to make him want to track the surgeon

down and break a few of his fingers. He could feel for the guy after what he'd been through with his daughter, but for him to blame Theresa…

"He was wrong to blame you. He should have known better and that he didn't—well, just goes to show he doesn't deserve you."

Her blue eyes shimmered with tears as she met his gaze. "I never thought of it like that before. Never asked myself how I would feel if Michael had been the one driving. I still would have wanted to do everything in my power to help Natalie—to help both of them heal."

And her ex had robbed her of that chance. How much of Theresa's fear about returning to the ER was tied to that loss? Yes, her physical limitations were holding her back, but the emotional obstacles were surely just as much of a hurdle to overcome.

After all, if she couldn't help Natalie, if she couldn't "fix things" with Michael—two people she'd loved—how could she help patients who were total strangers?

"I'm sorry you didn't get that chance. I—I know what it's like to see someone you love lying in a hospital bed. How helpless and useless it makes you feel when you realize there's nothing you can do to help them."

Sympathy softened her expression, wiping away some of the pain and sorrow of her own past. "Your father?"

Jarrett nodded stiffly. He didn't want this to be about him, about his family. "Helping Natalie and Michael might have given you some sense of closure about the accident, but there is nothing wrong with wanting Natalie to get better." He ran his hand across her shoulder and down her arm, giving her hand a gentle squeeze as if he might convince her with his actions should his words fail. "Nothing wrong with *you* wanting to get better, with wanting to go back to the job you love or with wanting to help other people heal."

Her throat worked as she swallowed. "Thank you, Jarrett."

He nodded again, cutting off a teasing comment about his willingness to slice open his hand anytime. The moment was too…important, too special to joke about. Too special, too important, too *intimate* even, he thought, to throw desire into the mix. So despite Theresa gazing up at him—her dark hair tumbling around her shoulders, her blue eyes wide and soft, pink lips slightly parted—silently asking him to kiss her, he ignored that plea.

Ignored, too, the almost desperate urge to pull her body tight to his, to feel the softness of her curves, breathe in more of the rain-kissed, wildflower scent of her skin as he captured her mouth with his own.

Instead, he sucked in a deep breath and held tight to his control. Leaning close, he gently brushed his lips against her forehead as he murmured, "You're welcome."

Chapter Ten

On Friday evening, Theresa was touching up the last of her makeup as she readied for Drew and Debbie's wedding when her cell phone rang. She smiled as she picked it up and saw the picture of her best friend smiling back at her. "Caitlyn, how are you doing?"

"A question I should be asking you!" Her voice dropping to a teasing whisper, she asked, "What's this I'm hearing about a sexy cowboy?"

Theresa's jaw dropped. Her cousins had long complained about the small-town grapevine and how no secrets stayed secret for long, but she never would have thought the information would travel all the way back to St. Louis. "How— Who—"

"Alex had a grumbled complaint or two about the guy you're staying with."

Theresa didn't bother to explain her temporary living arrangement. And she was more interested in the fact that her brother had called Caitlyn—even if it had been to discuss his little sister's love life with her best friend. She knew better than to tease Caitlyn about the call. The poor girl had been in love with Alex since they were kids. Shame her brother was too focused on the bad guys to see the great girl standing in front of him.

"I probably don't even want to know what Alex said, but I can pretty much assure you that he has it all wrong."

"Well, I told him if you wanted to have a vacation fling with your hunky cowboy, you should go for it."

Her friend's words inspired a burst of laughter. "I can just picture the look on his face!"

"I know. Total bummer that I didn't get to tell him in person."

"I wish you could have come with me." As a teacher, Caitlyn had to limit her vacations to summer break, but they had long talked about her coming to Clearville to see the sights in the small Victorian town and to hang out with Theresa's cousins, whom she'd met over the years as they visited Theresa's family in St. Louis.

"Maybe next time," Caitlyn offered. "So what are you up to?"

"At the moment, I'm getting ready for the wedding."

"Oh, I should let you go."

"It's okay. I have time." It still took her longer than usual to do everyday chores when so much of the time she had to work one-handed and had planned ahead. "I don't have to leave for another fifteen minutes or so."

"How are you doing? And I don't mean physically because I know how sick you are of those questions. I mean, how are you with the wedding? It has to make you think about Michael and...everything."

Everything being the ceremony the two of them had planned.

"I know it will bring back memories, but I'm going to do my best to focus on Drew and Debbie. This is their day, and I really am happy for them."

Though not part of the official bridal party, Theresa had attended the rehearsal dinner the night before. Seeing her cousin—all of her cousins—so in love had brought an ache to her chest, but her thoughts hadn't immediately turned to her ex-fiancé.

Instead, she'd thought about Jarrett.

Ever since the night at his office, she'd felt as though he'd helped lift the weight of guilt from her chest. For so long, she'd viewed the accident through the shattered glass of the driver's seat, but Jarrett had given her a different perspective.

If Michael had been driving the car that day, would you be any less concerned about Natalie's recovery? You've dedicated your life to helping people. I don't have a single doubt that you would have done anything to protect Natalie.

Though her heart still ached when she thought about Natalie, Theresa had to take comfort in knowing the little girl's health was improving and that Michael had hired the best nurses and therapists to help his daughter. Blaming herself wouldn't do Natalie—or herself—any good, and as much as she could, Theresa wanted to put the accident behind her.

"I'm just going to focus on having a good time. Let the past be the past and not think too much about the future."

A weighted silence filled the line before Caitlyn gasped, "Oh, my gosh! You really are thinking about having a fling with your cowboy!"

"Caitlyn!" A bright blush flooded her face, even as she made the protest, and Theresa could only be glad her friend wasn't there to see. "How did you make that kind of a leap from anything I just said?"

"Letting go of the past? Not thinking of the future? That has red-hot fling written all over it!"

Red-hot fling... Another surge of heat shot through Theresa as she remembered the way Jarrett had kissed her the night of Debbie's bachelorette party—and how eagerly she'd kissed him back.

She hadn't seen him much in the past two days since she'd bandaged his hand, but every time their gazes would meet—while he was working with one of the horses, as he and Chloe discussed an upcoming trail ride, while she was grooming Silver, who'd quickly become her favorite of all the horses—the awareness was there. The desire and need swirling around them like the dust motes drifting from the rafters in the warm spring sunlight.

But it wasn't something so simple as physical attraction. Theresa didn't know how many times she'd heard his words echo through her thoughts, encouraging and motivating her to do exactly what she'd told Caitlyn—to let go of the past and look to the future.

"So tell me more about this guy," her friend encouraged. "I have to admit, I thought Alex was so far off base, I really didn't pay that much attention. I thought it was all just big-brother overprotectiveness. Turns out maybe he was right to be a little worried, huh?"

"You make that sound like a good thing."

"It is. Alex needs someone to shake up his world and make him realize he's not the only one who gets to make all the decisions."

Maybe Alex did, but Theresa's own life had already been turned upside down. Did she really need anything more to shake up her life? "His name's Jarrett Deeks, and he's a former rodeo star. He was a bull rider."

As Theresa went on to fill Caitlyn in on what she knew of Jarrett's life—far less, she realized, than he knew of hers—she added, "He has this amazing way with horses... and people, too, though he tries to hide it. When he offered Chloe a job, he made it sound like she'd be doing him a favor, taking over the riding lessons, when it was just so obvious that he didn't have the heart to see her give up her horse."

"Sounds like he definitely has a way with *you* to have made such a big impression in such a short time."

Theresa's hand tightened on the phone. "But that's part of the problem. It has been a short time. I've only known Jarrett a little over a week. I'd be crazy to rush into something, especially when I'm leaving at the end of the month."

Caitlyn sighed. "Take it from a woman who's been hopelessly in love with your brother for *years*. Rushing doesn't sound like such a bad thing."

"Alex thinks Jarrett might just be a distraction."

Her friend gave an inelegant snort. "He would. But remind me why you are listening to your all-work, no-play brother when it comes to romance?"

"Because I can't help wondering if he's right," she confessed. "Spending time with Jarrett, taking care of the horses, it's been wonderful. A wonderful escape, but it's not real life. Everything I've worked for and planned for is back home. I keep talking about moving forward, and maybe by staying here, I'm only delaying taking those steps."

"But that's the thing about plans, Theresa. They change. Sometimes whether we want them to or not. The accident pushed you onto a totally different path, one that's led you to Clearville...and to Jarrett."

"You don't actually think it's fate that we've met, do

you?" And why did those words that she meant to come out so cynical sound so hopeful, instead?

"Maybe fate is what we make of it, and it's up to you to make the most of the time you have with Jarrett."

Jarrett had never been a big fan of weddings, and he still wasn't sure how he'd attended more ceremonies in the past year than he had in his first thirty-two years combined. Becoming friends with the Pirellis seemed to have something to do with it. Drew was the latest to wed, and Jarrett actually felt a twinge of sympathy for Theresa's brothers, who'd huddled together on the far side of the ballroom as if there was safety in numbers.

Jarrett wished them luck with that. If the same held true for these Pirelli brothers, they'd be falling like dominoes into wedded bliss one after the other.

"Hey."

Jarrett glanced over as Ryder Kincaid stepped up to the bar. He knew the other man in passing and that he'd been hired by Drew to take on some of the construction company's remodeling work. Though originally from Clearville, Ryder had only moved back recently, and the designer suit he wore was definitely a holdout from his San Francisco wardrobe. "Kincaid."

"You look about as uncomfortable as I feel," Ryder said after ordering a beer.

Jarrett gave a short laugh, even though he supposed it was true. He did consider the Pirellis his friends, but he hadn't gone out of his way to fit in with the rest of the small town. He was still—and perhaps would always be—considered an outsider. But Ryder— "This is your hometown. Figured you'd be welcomed back with open arms."

"Ten years is a long time. God knows I'm not the same cocky kid I was when I left."

Jarrett thought some of that cockiness remained. Why else would Ryder wear the thousand-dollar suit to a wedding where the rest of the guests would be in their Sunday best, bought off the rack at the closest mall?

"I'm sure Drew's glad you came."

"Yeah, he's a great guy and a good boss. Hope everything works out for him."

The wish might have been sincere, but the doubt came through loud and clear. "Not a fan of weddings, huh?"

"Been there, done that, lost the T-shirt in the divorce settlement. How about you?"

"Me? No, never been married."

"Ever come close?"

Close enough to still have some scars… He and Becca had talked about getting married, about the life they would have as they traveled together from one rodeo to the next. He'd never expected any woman to welcome that kind of transient lifestyle, but Becca had been a barrel racer, successful and popular in her own right, and she loved the rodeo life.

And, as Jarrett figured out following his accident, loved being with a rodeo star. When the doctors warned that he would never ride again, the news had sent Becca running. Oh, sure, she'd stuck around for a little while—maybe to try to make him feel better or maybe to simply make herself feel better—but in the end she still left.

Unable to stop himself, Jarrett glanced over at Theresa sitting at a table reserved for the groom's family. She looked stunning in a pale blue dress that was similar in style to the sapphire bridesmaid dresses. The bodice formed a twisted knot between her breasts, and the shimmery fabric floated to midcalf. The whole thing was held up by beaded straps that looked fragile enough to break beneath a heated glance and left her arms and shoulders completely bare. She'd taken his breath away from the moment he saw her, and he hadn't gotten it back.

Only a few more weeks and then she, too, would leave.

Not that circumstances were the same. Whether she chose to return to the ER or not, her life and career were waiting for her back in St. Louis. He was smart enough to know she wouldn't stay in the small town. Smart enough to know any relationship would be temporary.

Only a few more weeks… Instead of warning him off, the words urged him on.

"Sure you wanna go there?" Ryder asked, tipping his beer in the direction of Jarrett's gaze. "Theresa's got her whole family and half the town watching out for her."

Undeterred, Jarrett pushed away from the bar. If his years in the rodeo had taught him anything, it was how to focus on a goal and how to block out a crowd.

"Theresa, so good to see you again!"

"Don't you look wonderful?"

"I heard about that horrible accident, and we're all so glad to see you've fully recovered!"

Theresa's face hurt from forcing a smile in response to the many greetings from the wedding guests. They meant well, she knew. Their caring and concern was genuine, and if a hint of curiosity also fueled their questions, she supposed she couldn't blame them. It was, after all, a small town, where people made a point of knowing all there was to know about their neighbors.

Even temporary neighbors.

Getting through the actual ceremony hadn't been as difficult as she'd feared.

She didn't think she'd ever seen her cousin Drew look more handsome or happy than when Debbie stepped out from the back of the chapel and started her walk down the aisle. She'd looked stunning in a white satin gown, the fitted, strapless bodice covered in seed pearls in a floral pattern that trailed down to the full, floating skirt. Her blond hair was pulled up into delicate ringlets entwined with white rosebuds, and her makeup only served to highlight the happiness in her blue eyes and radiant smile.

Theresa had worried seeing the bride and groom standing at the altar, pledging their love and speaking their vows, would make her think of her might-have-been wedding.

But in truth, there was no comparison. Michael had never looked at her the way Drew looked at Debbie.

Her gaze drifted over to the bar and Jarrett. Though they had yet to speak that night, she'd been aware of his presence the whole time. Like most of the guests, he was casually dressed. She'd almost expected him to wear his typical jeans and cowboy boots since she'd never seen him in anything else. He *had* worn boots, but she would guess they were custom-made from the intricate pattern in the black leather, along with a pair of black slacks, a dark blue dress shirt and intricate silver bolo tie.

The simplicity of the clothes worked on him, nothing to distract from the broad shoulders, flat stomach and leanly muscled limbs. His rich brown hair gleamed beneath the hotel's amber sconces, and even from across the ballroom, she could feel the heat of his hazel gaze. He was standing at the bar with another man, but there was still an air of reserve surrounding him. No one would figure Jarrett as the life of the party, and she couldn't shake the feeling that he was simply there waiting.

For her.

"Theresa? Theresa?"

"Hmm?" Glancing over, Theresa realized her mother had asked a question. "Sorry, what were you saying?"

She might have lost track of the conversation, but she couldn't possibly miss the worried look her mother exchanged with her aunt. "Are you getting tired? Is this all too much for you? The rehearsal dinner last night and the wedding today—"

"It's fine," she interrupted. "I'm fine. Really."

"Your aunt was asking if you remember Marie Oliver," her mother repeated.

Forcing her attention away from Jarrett and toward the silver-haired woman standing nearby, an old memory flashed through Theresa's mind. Climbing one of the enormous trees in her cousins' backyard. Showing off and trying to prove the city girl was as adventurous and daring as her country cousins. Reaching for a high branch, missing, and the heart-stopping second when she knew she was going to fall.

"I do remember," she said suddenly. "You were the nurse at the clinic."

The older woman nodded. "Doc Crawford and I set your arm when you thought you were a little monkey, climbing that tree."

"I think it was more like some kind of superhero, but either way, I can't believe you remember."

"Oh, well, I've had plenty of opportunity to keep in touch with what's happening in your life through your aunt and uncle. For a while, I think they were in our office just about every other week with those three boys." Her gaze turned misty as she sought out Theresa's cousins. "Hard to believe they're all grown up now." Refocusing, Marie said, "I heard from your aunt that you're a nurse now, too. Any chance that I can take a bit of credit for that?"

Theresa laughed at the proud look in the woman's eyes. "Actually, I think you can. You and the doctor here were both so kind and caring, and it was like magic to me. That you had the power to make people feel better." And that was what being a nurse was all about, wasn't it? Whether working in an ER or a small-town doctor's office, the patients were the ones who mattered. "And of course, it didn't hurt that you gave me that really cool hot-pink cast."

"Always a popular fashion accessory for daring young girls," the nurse teased. Her expression sobered slightly, and Theresa sensed the woman's quick evaluation, looking for lasting injuries from the car accident. "So, you'll be going back to work soon?"

Her mother opened her mouth, no doubt to bring up the hospital administration classes Theresa hadn't signed up for and didn't want to take, but her aunt silenced her with a gentle touch.

"I haven't been medically cleared yet." Her plans for the future were as up in the air as when she'd arrived, but her conversation with Jarrett that night in the stables had opened her eyes. He'd made her realize her own feelings of guilt and loss were holding her back every bit as much as her physical limitations.

"Well, I'm sure I'll hear about it. Nick, Drew and Sam might have grown up enough to stay out of trouble, but there's a new generation of Pirellis now. We saw Sophia's darling boy for a checkup just the other week."

As the talk turned to the newest Pirelli grandchild, Theresa's thoughts stayed focused on Marie Oliver's words. What would it be like to follow a patient, not just for a few weeks, but from one generation to the next? To know not just their medical history, but so much of their life story?

Theresa had treated countless broken bones during her years in the ER, but as much as she hated to admit it, those patients quickly became nameless, faceless cases, known only by their injuries. The compound fracture in room one, the lacerated spleen in room two, the first-degree burn in room three.

That was part of the job, of course, and not something she should feel guilty about. She'd always thought an ER was the place she could do the most good, that the fast pace and sometimes hectic atmosphere was where she thrived...

Suddenly aware of the conversation around her coming to a halt, Theresa looked up in time to see Jarrett hold out his hand. The clean white bandage gleamed against his tanned skin. "Can I have this dance?"

Her mother made a soft sound, similar to the one she'd made when she saw the low-heeled but strappy sandals Theresa was wearing. *Are you sure that's a good idea?*

No, Mom, she thought to herself. *Not sure at all.*

But as she placed her hand in Jarrett's, a bad idea had never felt so good.

Chapter Eleven

"You do realize we've just opened ourselves up for a whole lot of questions from my family, don't you?" Theresa asked as Jarrett led her toward the dance floor.

"Yeah, I bet your brother will want to ask most of his questions with his fists."

"You don't sound too worried." And maybe he didn't need to be. Yes, Alex was used to chasing down bad guys, but Jarrett had made his living wrangling bulls. She didn't really think the two men would come to blows, but it just might be an even match if they did.

"Worried? Nah, some risks are worth taking."

Everything about Jarrett was a risk. Yes, she was an adult, but her family would worry about her rushing into a relationship with a man she'd known such a short time. She hadn't yet found a way to silence Alex's voice in her head, either. Was she just using Jarrett as a distraction? Trying to lose herself in a man she'd be leaving in only a few weeks? And if her feelings were something deeper, something more, didn't that pose an even greater danger?

As he pulled her into his arms, Theresa took an awkward, unsteady step. "I, um, haven't danced since the accident." Her leg was getting stronger, but she still had moments of stiffness when the muscles would tighten and refuse to give.

Not a problem at the moment, she thought as his palm slid to her lower back and he pulled her body closer to his. Heat spread from his palm throughout her limbs, threatening to melt muscle and bone and every bit of resistance within her.

A corner of his mouth kicked up in a smile. "Not a lot of call for it on the ranch, either."

The work he did with the horses was as graceful as a dance—the first few steps slow and deliberate as he gave the animals time to adjust, to relax and follow his lead. And maybe he had treated her the same way when she first arrived, but Theresa no longer feared he saw her as broken.

Almost as if he knew what she was thinking, he said, "I figure we make the perfect dancing partners—you lean on me, I lean on you. As long as we keep our feet moving, we can call it dancing."

It was what a relationship was supposed to be, wasn't it? Two people trusting in one another, balancing the other's strengths and weaknesses, turning to each other when times got tough.

With her right hand cradled securely in his palm, Theresa tentatively slid her left arm around his shoulders. Her muscles protested a bit, but not as much as they might have a few days ago. And with the right incentive... Since the accident, she had tried to do any number of tasks— braiding her hair, tying her shoes, holding a knife. The damaged nerves made all those actions awkward at best, impossible at worst, and she'd hated for anyone to witness those clumsy, frustrating attempts.

But as she cupped the back of Jarrett's neck, as her fingers slid into his rich, chestnut hair, she didn't feel the least bit clumsy. With the heat flaring in his eyes, the slight catch in his breath, she felt sexy, seductive…whole.

"How long do you have to stay at this thing?" His voice had dropped to a deep rumble, one Theresa could feel with her breasts pressed against his chest.

The vibration seemed to settle inside her heart, kick-starting the beat to an even faster tempo. "Not much longer," she said, even as the pulse pounded out a different answer. *Now. I want to leave now.* "You know, my family is always trying to get me to take it easy. Not to push myself too hard."

"So if you cut out of here early, to go back to the cabin and…relax, you'd really be taking their advice."

"Following doctor's orders, even."

And Theresa had always prided herself on being a model patient.

Even so, she wasn't able to slip away as quickly as she'd hoped. She'd planned to sneak out after the cutting of the cake, but her parents along with her aunt and uncle had wanted more family pictures taken. Unfortunately, their family was a large one, making the perfect shot with everyone smiling just right nearly impossible. Especially once her brothers and male cousins started goofing off, pulling faces and cracking jokes right at the click of the camera.

"Honestly, it's like they're all still twelve," Sophia complained, even as she reached over and held up two fingers behind Sam's head.

"Good thing you're much more mature," her husband, Jake, said wryly, their infant son cradled in his arms.

Theresa laughed but couldn't help shifting impatiently as the photographer reset for another shot. Jarrett had left not long after their dance, and she'd honestly thought she'd be on her way back by now.

What if he thought she'd changed her mind?

Had she changed her mind?

Could she really go through with this? She hadn't even known Jarrett for two weeks and in just over that amount of time, she'd be going back to St. Louis. Did she really want to make love with Jarrett when she was leaving so soon? Did she really want to leave so soon without making love with Jarrett?

Her shoulders fell on a sigh as the questions circled through her thoughts until she was dizzy.

Her eagle-eyed mother was quick to notice and asked, "Are you all right? It's been a long day, and with you wearing those shoes…"

After the accident, Theresa had promised herself that she wouldn't use her injuries as an excuse or as a crutch, and the last thing she wanted to do was worry her mother. Still…desperate times called for desperate measures. "I am getting a little tired."

The words weren't a lie, after all, and in the end, they worked like magic. The clowning around stopped, and soon the photographer had what he promised to be the perfect family portrait. Theresa said her farewells to Drew and Debbie, who were heading out on their honeymoon and wouldn't be back before Theresa returned to St. Louis, and promised to see her parents and brothers before they headed home.

She actually thought she might make her escape when Sophia sidled up next to her. "Well, I know why Drew and Debbie are so anxious to get out of here, but what about you? Could it have something to do with a certain cowboy waiting for you back at the ranch?" she asked with a smirk.

"You heard my mother. It's been a long day, and I chose inappropriate footwear." Her teasing didn't last as she confessed, "I'm not sure what to do, Sophia. I…care about Jarrett, but how stupid am I to start something when I'm leaving so soon?"

"You're not stupid. You're one of the smartest women I know, but sometimes I think you play things too safe." When Theresa opened her mouth to protest, Sophia beat her to the punch. "How long did you and Michael date before you slept with him?"

Theresa sighed. "Point taken."

"Look, I'm going to give you the best advice I can. Follow your heart."

"You make it sound like I'm falling in love with him. But I'm not. I can't be."

"I hate to break it to you, Theresa," her cousin said with a sympathetic smile, "but I know you too well. If you're thinking about sleeping with Jarrett, you're not falling. You're already there."

Sophia's words followed Theresa all the way back to the Rockin' R. With each passing mile, her panic grew. Love Jarrett? It couldn't be true. Sophia was still a newlywed with a gorgeous husband and a beautiful baby. She had stars in her eyes that made her see happily-ever-after where none existed.

Theresa cared for Jarrett, of course. But it didn't have to be love. Didn't have to be forever. Didn't have to mean her heart would break when she left him behind.

The car's headlights cut through the darkness as she turned down the gravel road leading past the stables. She wasn't surprised to see the doors open and the lights glow-ing from inside. Naturally, Jarrett would want to see to the horses first. His connection to the animals in his care was just one of the things she...*liked* about him.

Oh, hell. Maybe she was just fooling herself, but when she caught sight of him through the open doors, still wearing his dress clothes from the wedding, standing outside Silverbelle's stall and running a hand down the shy horse's nose, she couldn't have driven by.

She made her way carefully across the ground. Her mother had probably been right about the shoes, but Theresa had known she'd be sitting for most of the wedding and reception. She hadn't expected a late-night trek out to the stables when she slid the strappy sandals on early that evening.

Her knees wobbled a bit, but that could just have easily have been because Jarrett had turned to watch her approach. His heated gaze followed her every step, and when she would have stopped a foot or so away, he caught her around the waist and pulled her as close as he had on the dance floor. Closer even as he ducked his head to breathe in the scent of her perfume.

"Did I tell you how gorgeous you look tonight?" he murmured in her ear. "Way too fancy for these stables."

"You're looking pretty fancy yourself." It was hard to imagine Jarrett looking better than he did in a Western shirt and denim jeans, but the dress clothes were a sexy change. The dark blue shirt brought out more of the green in his hazel eyes along with flecks of gold that glowed as he gazed back at her.

"At least I still have boots on."

"Something tells me you always have boots on," she teased.

"Not...always."

Her face heated at the implication, but she still didn't

look away. She wanted those boots off. Wanted *everything* off. A desire that must have been written across her features for Jarrett to see as he all but groaned her name a split second before he claimed her mouth with his.

He tasted like rich, decadent chocolate and bright, bubbly champagne, and she answered his kiss like a woman starved. She couldn't get enough, craving even more, and yet she sensed Jarrett holding back. The control that had been such a turn-on the first time they kissed became a frustration.

Breaking away, she caught his handsome face in her hands as she stared up at him. "I'm not that fragile, Jarrett. Don't touch me like I'll break. Like I'm broken."

Like a buzzer at the starting gate, her words released him. He kissed her again, giving desire free rein as his tongue tasted and explored, urging her on with an advance-and-retreat rhythm that had her melting against him. His hands moved from the relative safety of her waist to more dangerous territory, one curving over her hip, pulling her as close as the narrow skirt of her dress would allow. She arched her back, clinging to his arms and gasping at the heat and strength of his arousal. Startled, really, by just how much he'd been holding back…

At first, the low rumble of sound blended into the moment. A vibration of need and desire growing stronger, closer, louder… Only after Jarrett pulled away with a ragged gasp did Theresa finally realize what she was hearing.

"Expecting someone?" she asked as she struggled to catch hold of her breath and her runaway desire. She slid the strap of her dress back in place as if a dozen sparkly beads on a piece of string would shield her from the hunger in his gaze.

Jarrett's wry smile played at odds with the heat in his

eyes. "Not unless Alex has decided to come save you from yourself."

"He wouldn't go that far." Theresa laughed shakily, even while she hoped it wasn't her brother driving up to the stables. No way would Alex miss the telltale signs of what had just happened—Jarrett's rumpled hair, the touch of lipstick on his mouth, his untucked shirt. But after Jarrett straightened himself up as best he could and headed toward the doors, she heard him swear beneath his breath and realized it wasn't one of *her* relatives climbing from the rental car parked outside after all.

"Summer...what the hell are you doing here?"

As Theresa walked down to the stables the next morning, she had a hard time ignoring the concern echoing in every step along the way. Jarrett hadn't said much following Summer's arrival the night before. At first, Theresa wanted to believe the surprise had simply caught him off guard. But the long—and lonely—night had given her too much time to wonder if his silence and withdrawal might have had more to do with what the two of them had been doing before his sister's interruption.

But as she stepped inside the cool building, it wasn't Jarrett she saw walking along the stalls.

"Morning." Jarrett's sister greeted her with a bright smile.

His sister... Theresa still wasn't sure what she might have expected Summer to look like—or sound like—but she had yet to figure out how a Midwestern rancher and cowboy had a Southern debutante for a sister.

Half-sister, she remembered, as he'd quickly pointed out during their brief introduction last night.

With her honey-streaked brown hair caught up in a ponytail and her face free of makeup, Summer Carrington looked right at home in the stables. And not nearly as out of place as she had the night before standing in the middle of Jarrett's rental office as he carried in her designer luggage. She'd traded in her off-white silk pants and peach cashmere sweater for boots, jeans and a riding jacket, making her offer to help Jarrett with the stables and the horses not seem quite so unbelievable in the light of day.

Wondering if Jarrett had come to that realization, too, Theresa said, "Morning. Did you get all settled in last night?"

Summer wrinkled her nose as she made a face. "Not exactly. Jarrett's already warned me not to unpack since he says I won't be stayin'."

"I think you caught him a little off guard."

"I know." She kicked at some loose straw with the toe of her boot. "But if I told him I was comin', he would have said no anyway. So at least this way, I get to see him even if it's just for a day or two."

Her heart aching at the longing in the younger woman's eyes, Theresa tried to rein the emotion in. She didn't know the whole story here. Heck, she probably didn't even know half the story. For all the talking she'd done about her family and her past, Jarrett had remained tight-lipped about much of his. Other than the one night when he opened up about his accident. He'd let down some of the walls around him then, and she'd let down her guard.

She'd kissed him that night. But more than that, she'd started to fall for him...

Swallowing hard against the thought, she asked, "Have you had a chance to talk to him this morning?"

Summer shook her head as she reached out to pet Duke. The horse welcomed the newcomer like an old friend, nudging her shoulder to encourage Summer to keep up the good work. "He was already gone this morning. I met a girl on the way in—Chloe? She said he called her to come out first thing to handle the riding lessons."

A touch of color highlighted her cheeks as she said, "I didn't know that he'd rented out the first cabin."

Theresa had joked about Jarrett sleeping in the stables. She hadn't been far off. It turned out he had a small bedroom tucked behind his rental office, which he'd given up to Summer the night before. Theresa hadn't asked where Jarrett planned to sleep once he made the offer to his sister. Her conscience had been too busy mocking her with the possibility of where *she* might have spent the night if not for Summer's arrival.

"I have family in town for a wedding that took place last night. Most of them are leaving this afternoon, and I have relatives that I could stay with..."

"Oh, no. Please don't!" Summer looked slightly horrified by the offer. "If you leave, Jarrett will never forgive me."

"I'll be leaving soon enough anyway," Theresa said, a reminder far more for herself than for Summer.

"But not on my account," the other woman argued, the speculative look in her eyes making Theresa wonder how much she and Jarrett had given away the night before.

Eager to change the subject, Theresa said, "Jarrett mentioned that you're from Georgia?"

Summer nodded. "Born and raised outside of Atlanta."

"And Jarrett?" Theresa instantly bit her tongue, but the words she had no intention of saying were already out.

Summer laughed as if she knew at least part of what Theresa was thinking. "*Not* born and raised in the South. When my mama was married to Jarrett's daddy, they lived all over the place—Montana, Wyoming, Colorado, New Mexico."

What was that like, Theresa wondered, for Jarrett as a

child? Was the somewhat transient childhood the reason for the distance she sometimes sensed?

It's not easy for me to let someone take care of me.

Had that constant uprooting during his childhood taught him he could only rely on himself? The questions only reminded her how little she did know about Jarrett. Too little to have gotten so carried away the night before. And while she didn't want to pump Summer for information, the younger woman was all too ready to share. "After they got divorced, my mama married my daddy and a year later I was born."

Guessing Summer to be in her early twenties, Theresa figured Jarrett must have been very young when his parents divorced. From what he had told her of his past, he'd been close to his father. But he hadn't mentioned his mother. At all.

"Growing up, Jarrett used to spend summers with us. At least he did until he turned eighteen. After that, well, I guess since he was an adult, no one could make him."

Shocked, Theresa asked, "You haven't seen him since he was eighteen?"

"No, he came back after, but…" Summer's voice trailed away, and she dropped her gaze, looking for the first time as if she'd revealed too much. She gave a small laugh. "Looking back, I'm surprised he came for those summer visits at all. He never was real good at doing things he didn't want to do."

As Summer gave Duke a final pat and glanced around at the rest of the stables, she said, "He was in the rodeo, did you know that?"

Theresa nodded, at once relieved and disappointed that this bit of information was something Jarrett had already shared with her. "A bull rider, yes. He told me."

"I saw him ride once." A hint of awe filled Summer's

voice—like a teenage girl who'd had the chance to see the hottest pop star in concert. "He was competing in Jacksonville, and I told my parents I was spending the weekend with a friend. You should have seen him, Theresa. I know the ride didn't last more than a few seconds, but it was like I'd watched it in slow motion. It didn't seem possible for him—for anyone—to hang on to a bull twisting every which way. But he did. He won that day, and I was there to see it," she added with pride, as if her presence had somehow contributed to the victory.

"Of course, I ended up getting caught by my parents. And then I got in even more trouble when I refused to tell them where I really went that weekend." Her ponytail flipped over her shoulder as she glanced at Theresa with a smile. "But it was worth it."

"Seeing Jarrett?" Theresa asked. "Or sneaking away without your parents knowing where you were going?"

Summer laughed. "Both, I suppose!"

"Do they know where you are this time?"

Both women jumped at the sound of the masculine voice at the doorway to the stables. Summer made a face as she turned to look at her brother. "Yes, they know. Not that I'm a kid anymore or need to tell them where I'm going."

"I bet your father wasn't too happy about it, though, was he?"

Ignoring that, Summer said, "Mama thought it was a great idea. In fact, as soon as you have another cabin ready, she'd love to come visit—"

"Forget it, Summer."

His sister sighed, disappointed but undaunted as she pressed on, "All right. But at least let me stay. I can help. I know I can. I have my inheritance from Gram Carrington, and I've been wanting to do something good, something important with the money, J.T.—"

But Jarrett's expression hardened, his gaze turning cold. "If you want to stay, stay. But I don't want your money, Summer. I don't need it."

Grabbing hold of the reins, he led Duke out of the stable. The echo of his words and the strike of the horse's hooves on the concrete lingered in the silence left behind.

Summer heaved a breath "That went about as well as I expected."

"I'm sorry, Summer," Theresa said, aching and *angry* at the hurt she saw in the younger woman's face. "He's just…"

"He's my brother," she filled in when Theresa's frustrated words trailed off. "You don't need to explain him to me."

Maybe not, but Jarrett certainly needed to explain himself. Marching after him, Theresa ignored Summer's pleas to stop. How could he be so cold when all his sister wanted to do was *help*? How could he just turn his back and walk away as—as Michael had turned his back and walked away from her?

She stepped out of the dimly lit stable and squinted against the morning sunlight. Blinded by the glare…by the memories.

All she'd wanted was a chance to help Natalie—to help all three of them—heal after the accident. She'd desperately wanted to believe something good could come from the tragedy. That they would pull together as a family and be that much stronger for overcoming this hurtle life had thrown in front of them.

I don't want *your help, Theresa. Don't you think you've done enough already?*

Her eyes adjusted well enough for her to see Jarrett crouched beside Duke, checking the horse's shoe, but the ache was still there, low in her gut, and she crossed her arms at her waist as she approached him. "All she's looking for is a chance, Jarrett. Why can't you give her that?"

Letting go of the horse's leg, Jarrett stood and brushed his hands against his denim-covered thighs. "I don't need her help. I started this rescue on my own with *my* inheritance. I don't need her family's money."

"This isn't about helping you with the horses. Can't you see that?" Lowering her voice as she stepped closer, she said, "Summer is *your* family! She wants to be a part of your life. She loves you and—"

"She's a spoiled rich kid with too much time on her hands. You heard her back there. She's got more money than she knows what to do with, so she thinks she's going to turn me into her latest charity case. She'll be bored out of her mind in a few days, and she'll be taking her big ideas and her big bank account back to Atlanta. Which is exactly where she belongs."

"You don't know that."

"*I* don't know that? What do you know about any of this, Theresa? This isn't your family."

Theresa flinched. His words stung her heart, but a part of her still wanted to stand firm. To fight back and argue that he was wrong. If he would just open his eyes and see how much Summer cared—

How much *she* cared…

But Theresa already made that stand before. She'd pushed with Michael, always wanting more than he'd been willing to give, always trying to be a bigger part of his world, only to end up left behind and forgotten as he moved on without her. For far too many years, she'd chased after him, settling for crumbs of affection when her heart and soul were starving for the whole cake.

Not again. *Never* again.

"You're right. It's none of my business. After all, I'm nothing but a guest here. I won't make the mistake of forgetting that again."

Chapter Twelve

The whine of the drill cut off as Jarrett sank the final screw into another piece of drywall. He wished he felt some sort of satisfaction, but it was one piece when he had who knew how many left to go. And after the drywall, he still had to patch the screw holes, tape the seams and finish off the corners. Then there was baseboard to install, and the walls to prime and paint.

Your idea, remember? his conscience taunted. He'd instructed Drew Pirelli to leave the cabins unfinished. The contractor's crew had built the exterior and completed the plumbing and electricity, but Jarrett had wanted to put the final touches on the structures himself.

He was not rushing to finish so his half sister would have a place to stay. The work needed to be done if he wanted all of the cabins up and running by the beginning of spring as he'd planned. He'd let himself get behind and needed to take advantage of the free time he had.

Thanks to Summer.

He'd known his half sister was good with horses. She'd been riding her daddy's world-class Thoroughbreds since she could walk. He also knew George Carrington hired the best trainers and stable hands money could buy to handle the dirty work. He was sure Summer was never expected to saddle her own mount—let alone grab a shovel and muck out the stalls.

But as he'd overheard the other morning, his little sister evidently liked doing the unexpected.

When he'd bluntly refused her offer of help, he'd thought that would be the end of it. That Summer would stay a day or two, realize how bored she was without her friends around and so far removed from any kind of nightlife or shopping to keep her occupied, and head back to Atlanta.

Instead, she'd been at the stables every day, helping care for the horses, laughing with Chloe and charming everyone who came for trail rides or lessons. She'd brought a camera with her and took pictures of every guest astride their horse. She had a running list of email addresses so she could forward the photos along with updates about goings-on at the Rockin' R, a great idea Jarrett wished he'd thought of.

She worked hard and seemed determined to prove… something.

I saw him ride once.

The drill's high-speed motor drowned out all sound around him, but nothing was loud enough to block the echo of his sister's words. He'd had no idea she'd snuck away to see him ride. The events were usually too packed for him to spot a single face in the crowd, and she hadn't tried to track him down afterward. Probably because she knew how he'd react.

He swore as he sank the next screw too far into the drywall. Dammit, he shouldn't feel guilty about this! Summer had shown up out of the blue. What did she expect?

All she's looking for is a chance. She wants to be a part of your life.

He felt another swift kick in the gut when he remembered the wounded look in Theresa's blue eyes. He'd hurt her, and that was the last thing he wanted to do, but she couldn't possibly know how hard it was for him to be around Summer. How just the sound of her voice could jerk him twenty-plus years into the past. To a time when it had been his mother's sweet, Southern drawl saying his name.

J.T., honey, what'd ya'll do in school today?

J.T., wash up for dinner now.

Don't worry about that nasty nightmare, J.T. I'm right here...

And then the silence. His mother's voice was gone. She was gone, and that was the end of the boy he'd once been.

It wasn't Summer's fault that she sounded like their mother or that she looked almost exactly like Lilly at that same age, Jarrett knew, thanks to the dozens of photos his father had from their brief marriage. Photos Ray had refused to throw away even though they were all that remained of the woman he'd loved. The woman who'd walked away and left everything—including those photos—behind.

He would have just as soon forgotten all about her, the way she'd forgotten him, but it didn't work that way. At least not according to lawyers and judges and courts of law. To this day, he wasn't sure who his mother had been trying to punish with those mandatory summer visits—herself or him. Only thing he knew is that they were all miserable during those months.

Except maybe Summer. She'd always welcomed him with a sunny smile, oblivious to the resentment and tension that filled the air along with the 90 percent humidity.

He set the drill aside and reached for another large rect-
angle of drywall. A spasm ripped across his back at the
sudden movement. His breath caught in his lungs on what
would have been a curse if he'd been able to get the word
out. Instead, everything in his body tightened, every muscle seizing and turning to stone.

Working too hard...Theresa had warned him. But he
was going to get these cabins finished, and he was going
to do it on his own. His own blood, sweat and tears, he
thought, wishing that was more a turn of phrase than a reality. And with his own damned money.

I only want to help, Summer had told him again after
apologizing for her offer. And maybe she did, but her help
came with too many strings attached to her daddy's fat
wallet, and Jarrett had sworn he would never take money
from her old man again.

The pain started to ease to a level that at least made
movement possible, and he slowly pushed away from the
wall. Each motion was slow and tentative as he waited for
the lightning-quick spasm to strike again. He sank down
against the sawhorse and leaned forward, trying to take
some of the pressure off his spine and stretch out the muscles that had made their protest to the hard work known
in such spectacular fashion.

After a while, all that remained was the dull ache he'd
gotten used to over the years. A reminder of the past and
of a life he'd left behind. Maybe he'd eventually get used
to the other pain, too—the one in his chest whenever he
thought of Theresa.

She hadn't been down to the stables since their argument, and her absence made him realize how quickly he'd
gotten used to seeing her every day. How he'd looked forward to hearing her voice as she greeted each of the horses
with a gentle word and a soft stroke along their muzzles.

And for the first time, instead of thinking of the time he and Theresa had to spend together before she left, Jarrett started to think about the time he'd have to spend alone once she was gone.

Theresa wanted to deny how her heart leaped at the knock on the door, but the rapid pounding—in her chest, not at the door—made it impossible. She hadn't seen Jarrett since the day at the stables, and she'd started to wonder if they would talk again before she left. Every time she pictured handing over the keys to the cabin and having him thank her for her stay, her throat started to ache with unshed tears.

But she'd told herself she wouldn't push, wouldn't chase after him the way she had—emotionally, at least—with Michael. It would be up to Jarrett to make the next move...

She tossed aside the book she'd been trying to read and forced herself to walk slowly to the door. She even took a moment to smooth her sky-blue sweater over her denim-clad hips before opening the door.

"Hi!" Summer's bright smile held a hint of uncertainty. "I'm not bothering you, am I? I mean, you're a guest, and Jarrett would kill me if he knew I was here..."

All the more reason to welcome his sister inside as far as Theresa was concerned. Hiding her disappointment behind a smile, she said, "You're not bothering me at all. I was just reading, but I'd much rather have some company."

Relief brightened the younger woman's eyes. "Oh, good. After spending the last few days at the stables, I'd really love to talk about something other than horses."

"Come on in."

Summer looked around the small cabin as she stepped inside. "I was wondering what these cabins would look like inside. After seeing Jarrett's bedroom, I was kind of worried. Now I see I had good cause."

Trying not to think about how close she'd come to seeing the inside of Jarrett's bedroom the other night, Theresa still felt the need to defend the sparsely furnished cabin. "You have to remember this is the first cabin he's rented out and…"

Summer plopped down on the uninspired green couch. "Do you really think the others will be any better?"

Probably not, Theresa realized. "I don't think the people who stay here will want to spend much time inside, not when they have a chance to go hiking or fishing or riding."

"I'm sure you're right, which makes me wonder why you haven't been to the stables. Chloe said you were down there every day until I showed up."

"Sounds like you and Chloe have been talking about more than horses."

The young woman's grin was anything but repentant. "You and my brother might have come up in conversation." Her smile faded, though, as she said, "Jarrett's been miserable the past few days. At first, I thought he was still upset that I'd shown up, but now I think it's because he misses you."

Theresa wished she could believe that were true, but his absence spoke louder than his sister's hopeful words.

Reading the doubt in her gaze, the younger woman sighed. "Just think about it," she said. "Jarrett's not the type to make the first move when it comes to building bridges."

And Theresa wasn't willing to repeat the past, to be the one making *all* the moves.

Changing the subject, she asked, "Have you had a chance to see any of the town yet?"

"Just what I saw driving through, but I love all the Victorian buildings."

"There are a lot of fun little shops." Theresa hadn't missed the designer labels on the other woman's clothes— even the jeans and hoodie sweatshirt she wore today. "No big brand names, but some places to buy cheesy souvenirs, artwork and handcrafts made by the locals. And my cousin is the manager of a great antiques store on Main Street."

"Oh, I love vintage stuff. And I can't tell you how many antiques stores my mama and I have combed through, even though my daddy can't figure out why we like buying other people's 'junk.' I decorated my whole apartment with things I've found at antiques shops and— Oh, my gosh!" Bouncing to her feet, she declared, "We should do it. We should decorate this place!"

"Oh, Summer, I don't think that's a good idea."

"Just a few things. I promise not to go overboard." She waved a hand around the stark cabin. "You know this place could use a woman's touch."

Theresa didn't want to think about that. Didn't want to think about how *Jarrett* could use a woman's touch. She'd replayed the scene outside the stables a dozen times. In that moment, caught up in her own emotions, she'd missed some of his. She'd picked up on the anger and frustration easily enough, but hadn't she seen something else? Something older and darker. Tiny fragments almost lost in the midst of the noise and explosion.

This was about more than Summer showing up unannounced. More than a hardheaded rancher's stubborn refusal to accept help.

"You know Jarrett likely won't be too happy about us making changes in here," Theresa warned.

"I know. But he's not too happy now, either. At least this way he'll be angry but with a decorated cabin to rent out after you leave."

After she left... Theresa hated the way those words

- seemed to hollow out her insides, leaving her empty and aching. It had only been a few days, and she already hungered for the sound of his voice, the sight of one of his rare smiles. Maybe it was better this way. Get used to missing him now before it was time to leave for good.

He couldn't stay away.

Jarrett knew he should, knew it would be better for both of them if he kept his distance until it was time for Theresa to go. But everything his brain told him, his body ignored. Which is how he ended up at the front door of Theresa's cabin, hat literally in hand.

I'm nothing but a guest here.

She was more than that, and his gut twisted for making her feel like so much less. He owed her an apology and an explanation if he could work his way through it. Taking a deep breath, he knocked on the door and waited for Theresa to answer.

Wary blue eyes gazed back at him, and her voice was cool. "Jarrett."

Nothing less than what he deserved, but he couldn't help remembering the sound of his name on her lips in the heated moment before he kissed her. "Can I come in?"

For a second, she hesitated, and he thought she might just slam the door in his face. Instead, she stepped back and waved him inside a cabin he barely recognized. His jaw dropped a little at the changes around him. An earth-toned area rug softened the floor beneath the kitchen table, where a wooden bowl of fresh fruit sat between four place mats. Plump green-and-white-checked cushions decorated the hard-backed chairs, and matching curtains hung in the window.

Another rug stretched out in front of a couch made much more inviting thanks to a blanket folded over the arm and a few decorative pillows tucked in the corners. Western touches—a horse sculpture on the mantel, a cowboy hat hanging on the wall and a horseshoe above the front door—were a perfect fit for the ranch cabin, and the addition of two end tables, matching lamps and framed artwork completed the new look.

Theresa lifted her chin. "As long as I'm staying here, I thought I might as well be comfortable."

"And Summer had nothing to do with it?"

Lowering her defiant stance, she pulled one of the throw pillows off the couch and hugged it against her chest. She looked younger suddenly, vulnerable, and Jarrett felt like an ass. "If you decide you hate it, we can take it all back."

Hate it? Of course he didn't hate it. But the cabins were supposed to make money, not take money. A means to an end so he could further his efforts with the rescue. His focus—his love—was the horses and the stable, not the cabins.

"Theresa, I have five more cabins to finish and I can't—" Unable to admit the truth, he waved his hand around to encompass all the changes she and Summer had made. His shoulders slumped. "Hell, maybe I'm just fooling myself. Why would people pay money to stay in such bare-bones accommodations when so many other places are…more like this?"

"The property you have here—it's amazing. And as far as decorating the cabins, I'm sure your sister would love to give you a hand. She has great taste and a real eye for detail." Theresa laughed. "And she can bargain like she's down to her last dollar. You should have seen her, Jarrett," she added, even as her smile soon faded. "It would mean more to her than you could possibly imagine, if you'd just reach out to her a little."

A framed picture hanging over the fireplace mantel

caught his attention, and he ran his hand over the back of his neck as if he could wipe away the heat rising there. The candid shot caught him as he walked away from an arena, shoulders hunched, his Stetson pulled low over his forehead. He didn't know when the picture had been taken, but he'd clearly bitten the dust at some point. Dirt covered his jeans and shirt along with darker patches of sweat. He should have looked broken and defeated, but beneath the shadowed brim of his hat, the fading rays of sunset seemed to highlight the unrelenting determination written in his clenched jaw.

"Summer took that picture when she snuck away to the rodeo to see you ride."

"She— Really?"

"It's an amazing shot. The way she captured you so perfectly—proud, strong, stubborn."

Alone.

Theresa didn't say the word, but Jarrett felt it. In the picture and in the loneliness that had lived inside him since his father died. Somehow that isolation had always made him feel...safe until now. Until Theresa.

But old habits died hard, and he had to remember that long after Theresa went back to St. Louis and Summer returned to Atlanta, he'd have that loneliness surrounding him, so it probably wasn't the best idea to think he could just cast it aside.

With her blue eyes watching him so closely, though, the words started pouring out. "It's not pride. I know it probably seems that way, but it's not. When I first thought of starting a ranch, it was supposed to be me and my dad. Working together with our horses on our land instead of always working for someone else."

"But then he had his stroke?"

"Yeah, and I wanted to be there for him. To take care

of him, but I—I couldn't. With the medicine and the machines he needed just to keep him alive, he required around-the-clock care."

"*Professional* care, Jarrett. You can't blame yourself for not being able to care for him. You didn't have the training. That's not your fault."

The nurses and social workers had told him the same thing, but he'd still been struggling for a way, searching for a possibility, when his mother had shown up. He hadn't seen her in five years, and then he stepped into his father's hospital room and there she was. Seated by his dad's side, holding his unresponsive hand, as if she had every right to be there. As if she hadn't walked out on them years ago.

And while Jarrett might have forgiven his mother for leaving his father, he would never forgive her for showing up again after his father's stroke. But the social workers and doctors had been all smiles for his mother, saying how wonderful it was that Lilly was going to take care of Ray. Take care of everything...

His throat tightened in memory, making his words sound rough and hoarse, but he forced himself to tell Theresa the rest of it. "My dad had always been so tough, so strong. Even after my mother left, he stayed strong. And to see him like that, so helpless, was bad. But for my—for Lilly to see him that way and to see the pity in her eyes when she looked at him..."

He'd hated her in that moment. As a kid, he'd never understood what he'd done that made her leave him behind. And later, as a teenager, he'd been bitter and angry as hell that she'd continued the charade of them being one big happy blended family during those dreaded summers. But he'd never hated her—until that day in the hospital.

Anger and resentment and guilt still lived and breathed in his gut, like some monstrous three-headed dragon, over the way she'd charged back into their lives when Ray was at his worst. When he'd been unable to stand up to her or to tell her to go back to her Southern mansion, her old-money husband, and to leave the two of them the hell alone.

Jarrett had said all that and more, slamming the door shut in his mother's face, and vowing to the doctors and hospital social workers that he'd take care of his dad, the way Ray had once taken care of him.

Guilt breathed another round of fire, even at the memory of just how badly he'd failed to keep that promise. "I looked for rehab centers that I could afford, but even the least expensive was more than I could come up with back then. And those places—I wouldn't have left one of my horses in their care, forget putting my father there. And I knew Lilly could give him the best money could buy—round-the-clock nurses, daily therapy, treatments insurance might not cover. All of it. So in the end, I said yes."

"You did what was best for your father."

"Did I? Was it best for him or just easiest for me?"

Not that he hadn't paid in his own way. His stepfather had seen to that.

My money...my rules.

George Carrington had made it clear Ray's care was contingent on Jarrett falling in line. He'd quit the rodeo and moved back to Atlanta. He told himself he would have done it anyway, wanting to spend as much time with his father as he could. But that hadn't made him want to punch the smug look off his stepfather's face any less as he'd sat through family dinners and taken a job working at the old man's stables.

He'd swallowed his pride and put up with living under his stepfather's thumb for his father's sake, but Jarrett had learned his lesson. He would never take the easy way out again.

"The ranch, the stables, the rescue—I wouldn't have any of it if it wasn't for my father's life insurance policy. Even though he's gone, I feel like he's still looking out for me. And I want to make him proud, Theresa. I want to show him—to show *them*—I can do this on my own."

Theresa didn't need to ask to know who Jarrett was referring to. His family had done a number on his pride, and while part of her understood how much of his self-respect he'd tied into working the ranch on his own, she couldn't pretend his words didn't hurt her heart a little. She didn't doubt that he'd succeed, but when he did, who would be there for him to share in that success?

"I have to do this on my own. It's the only way I'll be able to look myself in the mirror each morning."

Theresa knew better than to argue against such determination. She should be glad, she supposed, that he'd opened up to her the way he had, but understanding the reasons why he held himself apart from the people around him only made that distance seem so much harder to bridge. "I get it."

Seeing the disbelief in his gaze, she insisted, "I do. You think you have to do this alone, but just remember one thing. It didn't start out that way, did it? The ranch was something you wanted to share with your dad. And I know it's not the same without him, but, Jarrett, there *are* other people who care about you."

For the moment their gazes locked, Theresa's heart pounded as she wondered how much he could read in her expression. Did he know how much she was starting to care for him? How much it hurt her to think of him pushing himself so hard and pushing everyone else away? The coward in her wanted to look away, to take a step back before she gave too much away. But if she wanted Jarrett to lower his guard, wasn't it time maybe for her to give up her own?

"Jarrett…" She whispered his name around the lump in her throat, fighting the fear that urged her to swallow the words before she said them, knowing she wouldn't be able to take them back.

His gaze cut away as he shifted. Reaching out, he ran a hand over the Western-themed throw Summer had draped over the back of the couch. "This is nice."

The moment was gone, and disappointment and relief turned head over heels inside her stomach. "Yeah, we thought so, too."

It wasn't much, that small admission, but enough for Theresa to reach out and cover his hand with her own. For a split second, she wished that he'd been on her other side. That it was her right hand instead of her left. But as she willed her fingers to close around his, she changed her mind. Hard-fought victories always tasted the sweetest, and when Jarrett turned his wrist and wrapped his strong, sure fingers around her slightly trembling ones, she couldn't imagine anything better.

"Thank you," she whispered, "for telling me about your father. For helping me to understand and for…trusting me with that part of your past."

"Do you trust me?"

"Yes, of course."

"Then come riding with me."

"Now?"

The smile he gave her reached right into her heart, pulling her closer as he tugged at her hand. "Now."

Chapter Thirteen

Theresa took a deep breath as she followed Jarrett into the stable. She knew it hadn't been easy for him to open up, to be so emotionally vulnerable. Far more frightening than the physical challenge confronting her. And she *did* trust him. The harder part was trusting herself.

What if she couldn't hold on to the reins? What if the weakness in her leg threw off her balance, and she couldn't keep her seat?

But of course, those were useless worries. Theresa knew it even before Jarrett stopped in front of one of the stalls, where a spotted mare named Molly stuck her head out for a piece of carrot. In the short time Theresa had been staying on the ranch, she'd gotten to know the horses. Overly friendly Duke, shy Silverbelle and sweetly mellow Molly, a favorite of the young girls who came for riding lessons. First timers who wanted nothing more than a slow circle around the corral.

Like sitting in a rocking chair on your front porch,
Summer had told one of the nervous guests in her friendly
Southern twang just the other day.

No, Theresa wouldn't need to worry about falling off
Molly. She wouldn't need a tight grip on the reins to keep
the horse in line or worry that a sudden move would knock
her from the saddle. *It's still riding. It doesn't matter that
it won't be the same. That it won't be like it was before.*

She'd tried not to feel angry or bitter or, worse, filled
with self-pity over the accident. In so many ways, she was
lucky to be alive. Lucky to even think about riding a horse.
That was key here. Enjoying the moment and not making
comparisons, not longing for what could have been.

"Hey, Miss Molly." Reaching out, she stroked the
horse's satiny muzzle almost as if in apology. *You're a
good horse. Slow and steady.*

Just what the doctor ordered. She'd been told not to push
too hard or expect too much, too soon from her therapy.
Slow and steady when what Theresa wanted was to fly.
To run, to jump, to escape the trapped feeling that still
overcame her at times when the simplest tasks took so
damn long.

"Ready?" Jarrett asked as he grabbed a bridle for the
mare.

"Sure. Let's go for a ride."

Maybe that had always been her problem—wanting
too much, expecting too much. Maybe the lesson she was
supposed to learn from the accident was to simply accept
what was and not hope for so much more. But as Jarrett
stepped closer, she swallowed as her heart pounded out a
crazy beat. She caught a hint of soap and aftershave, the
fresh, woodsy scents drawing her closer and tempting her
to breathe him in. She already knew how perfectly she fit

in his arms, how her mouth felt made for his kiss. And yes, she wanted more. Wanted everything.

Jarrett had hoped going for a ride would put a spark into Theresa's eyes. That she'd feel the same freedom, the same peace that he had only been able to find on the back of a horse. But he'd miscalculated with Molly. He knew it the instant Theresa stepped close to the calm horse.

His plan had been to take things slow, to give Theresa time to adjust to riding again. But she wasn't some little kid who loved the idea of horses more than the reality, and she wasn't some novice greenhorn, either. A city girl, yes, but one who knew her way around a stable.

One who knew her own mind.

I'm not that fragile, Jarrett. Don't touch me like I'll break. Like I'm broken.

She was ready for a challenge. She had her relatives to protect her, to keep her safe and sheltered. She didn't need him for that. She needed him to help her break free.

Resisting the urge to pull her into his arms, he instead stepped away. "Wait here a second."

He had planned to take Duke on their ride. Solid, dependable Duke, and he gave the horse a carrot as he walked by. *Not this time, buddy.*

Instead, he saddled Champion. Like Duke, Champ was Jarrett's horse, but unlike Duke, the big chestnut gelding was far too spirited for anything so boring as trail rides. Champ was the horse he rode when he longed for a sense of freedom and flying. The powerful connection of horse and rider racing against the wind. It had always been a solitary escape for him in the past. As Jarrett swung into the saddle, though, he couldn't help grinning as the big horse shifted beneath him, muscles bunched in anticipation. Today it was a ride he couldn't wait to share.

Theresa's blue eyes widened as he held out a hand. The surprise wasn't enough to disguise the spark of attraction. Her pulse fluttered at the side of her neck, and he had the sudden urge to press his lips to that very spot. A spot that would be within easy reach if she said yes. "Still trust me?" he asked.

"I thought—" She glanced over her shoulder at Molly. "I thought we were going on a trail ride."

"Up to you. You decide how fast or slow and how far we go."

A slow blush climbed her cheeks, but she didn't look away as she said, "I think we've gone slow enough already."

The softly spoken words nearly knocked him from the saddle and only when Theresa took a step back did Jarrett realize he'd unwittingly kicked Champ in the sides. He had the horse under control in seconds. Couldn't say the same for the desire racing through his veins. "Still ready for this?" he asked wryly.

Her laughter filled the stables as she said, "I can't wait."

Reaching down, he wrapped an arm around her waist and pulled her onto the saddle in front of him. Her warm curves fit perfectly within the circle of his arms, the cradle of his thighs. Her fresh, summery shampoo teased him, and he didn't even try to resist burying his face in her soft, sweet-smelling hair. He found that spot on her neck and spoke with his lips moving against her skin as he promised, "Time to fly."

Racing from the stables, he had a split second to catch the startled look on his sister's face turn to a smile as they sped by, mud flying from beneath Champ's churning hooves.

At one time, Theresa had considered herself something of a horsewoman. She'd taken lessons over the years, trained in an arena, but that experience was nothing compared to riding with Jarrett. Performance jumping was all about precision and control as horse and rider worked through a set course.

Racing across open ground with Jarrett and Champ was all about…letting go.

Even in the days before the surgery, she doubted she would have had the strength or experience to command the powerful horse. But with Jarrett's arm wrapped like a steel band around her waist and his broad chest at her back, the only worry she had was about falling for the strong, sexy cowboy himself.

And at the moment, even that felt…right. Destined, even.

Only a few days ago, she'd mocked her friend Caitlyn's idea that fate had brought them together, but now it was her friend's response that echoed through her thoughts.

Maybe fate is what we make of it, and it's up to you to make the most of the time you have with Jarrett.

Theresa had every intention of making the most of today. A joyous laugh escaped her, and Jarrett's arm tightened even more. She wasn't sure how long they rode before he slowed the horse to a stop as the dense trees lining the trail gave way to a long, narrow meadow.

Champ was breathing hard from the exertion, and Theresa realized she was, as well. Jarrett slid from the saddle before helping her down. He kept a grip on her waist, helping her stand, and for the first time since the accident, Theresa didn't care about the weakness in her legs. The ride had been worth it.

"Thank you," she said breathlessly as she braced her hands on his chest. The lightweight cotton of his shirt transferred the heat of his skin through the fabric, and her fingers instinctively curled, seeking out more. "That was amazing."

"You feeling all right? I know it wasn't exactly the trail ride you were expecting."

Theresa shook her head, realizing most of her hair had slipped from its ponytail. Reaching up, she pulled out the band and shook the rest of it free to fall over her shoulders. "It was better than I could have imagined. Kind of like my first time clearing a jump."

Despite the easy grin teasing his lips, his gaze darkened as he reached out to run his fingers through her hair. "First times can be pretty incredible."

Her pulse pounded in her veins at the promise in his eyes, in his touch. "Yes, they can be."

It wasn't the first time Jarrett had kissed her, but that didn't make the moment any less incredible as he caught her up in a kiss every bit as exciting and exhilarating as the ride they'd just taken. He'd given back a piece of herself she feared she'd lost and the preciousness of the gift wrapped around her heart.

For her. He'd done this for her. And it didn't matter how many trail rides he'd led or cowboy wannabes he'd instructed, this was about so much more than that. This was about sharing the pain of the past and finding a way to move forward, to move on to a far more promising future.

The first drop that fell from the sky was almost soothing against her heated cheek. And when Jarrett caught the dampness with his lips, the rain became a part of the kiss. Almost like a blessing sprinkled down from Mother Nature as the sweet scent of rain filled the air. But when the light drops started falling harder and faster, Jarrett broke away. His chest heaved as he tried to catch his breath, and his scowl was as dark as the clouds that had gathered overhead. "Storm came in outta nowhere."

Theresa smiled as she reached up to brush her thumb against his lower lip. "I'd say it's been brewing for some time."

He caught her hand, pressing his mouth against her palm, and an instant rush of goose bumps raced up her arm. But he only frowned at the slight shiver. "We need to go. We're going to get soaked as it is."

"I won't melt," she promised.

But Jarrett wouldn't be swayed. Without another word, they were back on the horse with Theresa wearing his hat and Jarrett wrapped around her like a human poncho. True to her word, Theresa didn't melt. But they were both drenched within minutes, and even with the combined body heat, that slight shiver had turned into chills as the cold rain poured down over them.

Champ raced through the rain like a champion mudder, and Jarrett bypassed the stables, guiding the horse straight to Theresa's cabin. He swung down from the saddle and swept her into his arms, not stopping until he'd carried her up the steps and beneath the sheltering porch.

She laughed a little as he set her down. Her sodden clothes were cold and heavy against her limbs, her hair soaked despite the hat she handed back to Jarrett. His hair was plastered to his head, water running in rivulets down the rugged planes of his face and clinging to his eyelashes.

A wry smile twisted his lips. "Not the cold shower I had in mind."

But Theresa hadn't been thinking of cold showers. From the moment Jarrett kissed her, she hadn't thought of stopping at all. And though she was freezing on the outside, inside that same fire still burned. "Come in with me," she whispered.

Heat flared in his hazel eyes as he took a quick step forward, his boot heels striking against the wooden porch, but then he stopped, his expression pained. "I can't. I have to take care of Champ."

"Oh, right. Of course." Her face heated at her willingness to forget everything—including the poor horse standing patiently in the rain—so long as it meant being in Jarrett's arms again. "In that case...hurry back?"

Jarrett grinned. "Wild horses won't keep me away."

Chapter Fourteen

Darkness still blanketed the bedroom when Jarrett awoke with Theresa in his arms. *Not a dream, then,* he thought with a smile as he ducked his head to breathe in the sweet floral scent of her hair and drew her body closer to his. Last night had really happened. The freedom of the fast-paced ride with Theresa in his arms, getting caught in the storm, her invitation back to her cabin…

He hadn't known what to expect when he rushed back to the cabin after rubbing Champ down and seeing to the horse's food and water. He'd hurried as fast as he could, but enough time had passed to make him wonder. Had Theresa changed her mind?

When she opened the door wearing nothing but a pale blue robe, he had his answer. Her hair was still damp, and her skin held a flush of warmth that told him she'd taken a shower while she waited. He wished he could have joined her and thought to himself, *Next time…*

And he was determined there *would* be a next time and a time after that and after that... Until Theresa left as he knew she would.

But he didn't let himself think of that as she reached out for him, concern written in her blue eyes as she touched his chilled skin. "Come in, quick! You're freezing!"

"Only on the outside," he promised as he shook the lingering rain from his hat.

But Theresa didn't seem to care about the puddle gathering beneath his boots or the trail of water as she pulled him over the threshold. Or about the dampness that seeped from his clothes and through her robe as she wrapped her arms around him and pulled his head down for a kiss.

She tasted as sweet and fresh and clean as she looked, and the desire pooling in his veins was enough to leave him light-headed and aching. But he wanted her to be sure. "I want you, Theresa. I want to make love with you."

She pulled back when he hesitated, seeming to realize he was waiting for her response. A small smile played around her lips as she said, "I don't open the door naked to just any man."

He caught the end of the tie knotted at her slender waist. "You're not naked."

"Not yet," she said before the teasing light in her eyes grew stronger and yet softer all at the same time. "I want you, too, Jarrett. Make love with me."

All it would have taken was one tug at the belt, and her gorgeous curves would have been on full display. But somehow that wasn't the way it happened. Instead, it was Theresa helping remove his clothes.

She ran her palms over his shoulders and arms as she pushed his shirt off and let it fall with a damp plop onto the entryway linoleum. He toed off his boots with ease, but his wet jeans were another story. They clung to his legs like a second skin, and he nearly fell on his face more than once as her "helpful" hands kept getting in the way. By the time he'd stripped down to nothing but his boxers, he forgot all about being cold.

Ever.

In his entire life.

And heat only burned that much brighter as he backed Theresa farther into the cabin, stumbling slightly as his feet tangled with his discarded jeans. He could feel her laughter—against his lips and inside his chest—and didn't even care. Hell, he wanted to laugh, too. He couldn't remember ever feeling so…happy. But first—

Theresa squealed when he scooped her into his arms, making sure to step over the last of his clothes as he carried her toward the bedroom. He had a vague notion that she and Summer had decorated this room, too, but his main focus was the queen-size bed and the woman he placed in the center of it.

Theresa's dark hair spread over the white pillowcase, and she gazed up at him with eyes as blue as the wide-open skies he loved. He'd been right about the robe. One tug on the tie and the soft material slipped away from even softer skin. He chartered the same path Theresa's had taken earlier, running his hands over her delicate shoulders and satin-smooth back, curving around her narrow waist and flat stomach and up to cup the soft weight of her breasts.

She arched into his touch, her nipples pebbling against his palms, pleasure written across her face. He lowered his head to take her into his mouth, her seductive scent filling him as she buried her fingers in his hair. He matched the tug and pull of his lips and tongue with the rise and fall of her ragged breathing, increasing the pace until she was crying out for more. He slid his hand between her thighs, and the silken dampness he found there almost did him in.

"Theresa, wait." He started to pull away. "I've got to—"

"Here," she whispered, opening her hand and holding up the condom she must have slipped from the pocket of his jeans moments ago.

Jarrett almost sank into her arms in relief. The thirty seconds it would have taken him to run back to his jeans in the other room would have seemed like a lifetime. "You are incredible."

"This is incredible," she responded, and he didn't have to ask what she meant. The heat between them, the sheer perfection of the way she opened for his kiss, for the slow slide of his body into hers. All of it incredible and better than he'd imagined as the first tremors shook her body, gradually growing stronger, more powerful, as she cried out, finding her release and urging him toward his own.

Incredible, he thought again as she turned in her sleep to burrow against his chest. Too good to be true and, deep down in his heart he knew, too good to last.

Though it was the last thing he wanted to do, Jarrett had slipped from Theresa's bed to dress and head down to the stables. He was working his way through the morning chores—at a record-setting pace, he had to admit—when he heard the brisk sound of approaching footsteps. Theresa's recovery had come a long way, but she still had the slightest limp in her step. After the ride yesterday and *everything* that followed, he worried that she might be a little stiff and sore and moving a bit slower than usual.

Don't touch me like I'll break.

He'd taken her at her word, though at times he'd tried to hold back, but she hadn't let him. Theresa wasn't broken. She was a strong, determined, desirable woman, and she didn't need a man to protect her. She needed one to… love her.

Love her?

The words were still stumbling through his mind like a newborn colt on shaky, uncertain legs as his sister's cheery greeting cut through the predawn silence. "Have to say I didn't expect to see you out here so early."

Jarrett immediately turned his attention back to laying out fresh hay for Duke and away from Summer's cheeky grin. No way was he discussing his love life with his little sister. "Chores don't do themselves around here."

He should have known that wouldn't be enough to discourage her. Rolling her eyes, she grabbed a bag of feed and got to work beside him just as she'd done every morning since she'd arrived. Unfortunately, her mouth moved just as fast as she did. "I think it's great that you and Theresa are together. I like her."

"She's not staying, Summer." He said the words as much as a reminder to himself as to his sister.

But Summer's gaze was all too knowing as she murmured, "But you want her to."

"Doesn't matter what I want." What mattered was what was best for Theresa. She'd come to the ranch to heal, to put the pieces of her life back together so she could put the accident behind her and move on.

I'm not that fragile, Jarrett.

No, she was strong now. Stronger maybe than she'd been before the car accident, and if he'd had anything to do with that, well, then that would have to be enough.

Summer stopped him with a hand on his arm when he would have moved on to the next stall. "Don't push her away, Jarrett."

"I don't push—" He swallowed the words before he could speak them because he knew they were a lie. He'd spent a lifetime pushing Summer away, but this time, she seemed determined to stick. "One of these days, you're gonna have to tell me why you're really here."

"Is it so impossible to believe I want to spend time with my big brother?" Despite the teasing, the light in her eyes dimmed, darkened by memories, and Jarrett's gut twisted. But the moment was over and done so quickly, he was left to wonder if he'd only imagined it as she went on to say, "I think the work you've done with the rescue is amazing, and I'd really like to be a part of it…if you'd let me."

Jarrett knew it was Theresa's influence that had him admitting, "You've done a good job here."

And it was his half sister's unrelenting eagerness that had her saying, "But I could do so much more, Jarrett, if you'd just let me. With the money I have—"

"Forget it. I'm not taking money from your family."

"Okay, ignoring that my family is your family, too, it's my money. My inheritance."

Which she received from her paternal grandmother, and Jarrett never had and never would accept the Carringtons as his family, but he didn't say that to Summer. Because, of course, she was a Carrington and yet she was also his sister. Hell, this whole family stuff was more of a complication than he wanted to deal with. It'd been so much easier when it was just him and his dad.

Easier. The word rang through his head. Maybe it wasn't supposed to be easy. Maybe family was something worth fighting for even when times were tough…

"I just want to do something good, something worthwhile with that money."

"Your mother's involved with dozens of charities back in Atlanta. You know she'd help you set up some kind of fund or scholarship in a heartbeat."

"But like you said, those are *her* charities."

"And the rescue is mine," Jarrett pointed out, even

though it was so much more than that to him. A tribute to his father. A second chance not just for the horses to find a new home, but one for him, as well. As he said the words, though, he could hear Theresa's voice in his head.

The ranch was something you wanted to share with your dad. But, Jarrett, there are other people who care about you.

Would it really be so wrong to let—to *ask* Summer to help? A part of him rebelled at the idea—the stubborn, hardheaded bull rider with a chip on his shoulder and attitude to spare. The man whose picture Summer had taken all those years ago. But he wasn't that guy anymore. The guy who didn't give a damn because he had nothing to lose.

Silverbelle nickered softly as he neared her stall, awaiting his approach when not long ago, she would have shied away.

Now he had so much riding on his shoulders. The rescue's future hinged on renting out the cabins, and he needed to do everything he could to see that they were a success. Everything including asking for Summer's help. "There is something you could do."

"Really?" Hope lit her eyes, her eagerness making Jarrett felt like the world's biggest jerk for not doing what Theresa had suggested all along and just reaching out a little.

"I saw the picture. The, um, one you took of me."

It was Summer's turn for embarrassment as she said, "Theresa wanted to use some of my pictures to decorate the cabin. I have them saved on my computer, and she picked that one. Did you want me to have some more printed for the rest of the cabins?"

"Um, no, can't say that I do. But I do want to update the ranch's website. I'd like to get more pictures up of the rescue horses and of the new cabins…once you get them decorated."

"I already have a ton of pictures of the horses. You can look at them and pick the ones you want to use. And—you're going to let me decorate the rest of the rooms? Yes! I cannot wait!"

"Don't get too excited. You're gonna have to work with a serious budget because we're using my money, not yours."

Summer didn't let his warning dampen her enthusiasm. "You'll be amazed with how much I can do. It's all about making the most of what you have."

Making the most of what you have.

That was definitely Jarrett's plan as he finished up in the stables and headed back to Theresa's cabin. The sky was only now starting to lighten, faint streaks of color softening the night sky, the promise of an entire day still ahead, but he didn't slow his pace over the muddy ground. He and Theresa might not have much time, but he was determined to make the most of it.

Desperate to make the most of it, if he were honest with himself. Once Theresa left, all he would have were his memories. So sue him if he wanted to pack a lifetime's worth into a two-week period.

Unless there was a way to put that time to better use. To take those two weeks and try to convince Theresa to stay. Not forever. Just for a little longer.

He nearly choked as he tried to swallow, his mouth suddenly bone-dry at the thought of asking her to stay. What had he told her as he pulled her onto the dance floor the night of the wedding?

Some risks are worth taking…

Yeah, big talk so long as he didn't have to put his words into action.

Would it really be so hard to ask? Just a few short words. *Don't go. Stay.*

They repeated on a loop—or like an echo—familiar and frightening as he opened the cabin's door. *Stay. Don't go.*

But as he stepped inside, he froze for a moment as he heard Theresa's voice from down the hall. Judging by the one-sided conversation, she was obviously on the phone, and Jarrett relaxed a little. No witnesses at least if he did decide to put himself out there.

Don't go. Stay.

So focused on what he wanted to say, it took a moment for her words to register, for him to realize he didn't have to ask the question when she'd already given him the answer.

"No, Mom, nothing's changed. I'm staying through the end of the month."

Nothing's changed... Okay, so he couldn't expect Theresa to go into detail with her mother about the night they'd shared, but to hear it dismissed as nothing...

He sucked in a breath that seemed to sear his lungs. The shock of the words slammed him to the ground as hard as any bull ever had, and he fell back on old habits. Moving slowly, taking stock, trying to figure out just how badly he was hurt and whether or not he'd live... And like in those days as he'd push to his feet, spitting out dirt and blood, he'd grab his hat, shake off the dust and tell himself he was fine.

So now he knew where he stood with Theresa, and that was a good thing. The only thing, he figured, that would keep him from falling.

"Thanks for helping me out with all of this," Summer said to Theresa as the two of them, along with Sophia, carted their latest purchases from The Hope Chest to the back of the truck they'd borrowed from Jarrett. "I know I promised Jarrett I'd stay within budget, but it'd be all too easy for me to go overboard without ya'll along."

"We can thank Sophia for that. I totally appreciate the 'friends and family' discount, but I think we can all agree that will be our secret." Jarrett had turned his sister loose on the cabins, but he'd made his stance on who was paying very clear. Theresa didn't want to do anything to rock the delicate balance between the siblings, but she couldn't resist helping out a little.

"My lips are sealed," Sophia said with a conspirator's smile as she placed a tightly bubble-wrapped-and-boxed lamp in the nearly full truck bed. "And I love the cross-promotion idea you came up with," she told Summer, referring to the younger woman's idea to have flyers for The Hope Chest on display at the ranch along with a link for the shop on the new website. "As soon as you have the new Rockin' R brochures printed, let me know, and I'll start passing them out to all our customers."

"I just have a few more changes to make before they go to the printer. I can't wait for you to see them. And you'll have to come out to the ranch, too, so you can see all this in one of the cabins instead of in the back of a truck," she said with a laugh as she headed back inside.

Summer's enthusiasm was contagious, and Theresa couldn't help smiling. But then again, she'd been doing a lot of that recently. Something her sharp-eyed cousin had certainly noticed.

"I think I do need to take a trip out to the ranch. See for myself what's put the spark back in your eyes," she teased.

"Must be all the fresh air," Theresa said blandly.

"Uh-huh. And Jarrett has nothing to do with it?"

Theresa fought to keep her smile in place. Casual, friendly, no reason to break into a huge grin or worse, burst out in song, just because Sophia had said his name.

Only a few hours away, and Theresa couldn't wait to rush back into his arms. To see him smile and hear him laugh. To watch his eyes light up in greeting and darken with desire. To know all she had to do was walk by within arms' length for him to reach out and pull her into his embrace.

But she hadn't lied to Sophia about the fresh air. Jarrett was in his element in the outdoors, and Theresa loved being part of his world. They'd gone horseback riding almost every day—sometimes riding double on Champ, other times leading trail rides on Duke and Molly. She'd been wrong when she thought riding the calm, gentle mare wouldn't be enough. As it turned out, little could compare riding side by side with Jarrett at a pace slow and easy enough for them to hold hands and even share a stolen kiss or two.

Jarrett had given her a tour of the unfinished cabins and shared his vision for the ranch's future. His hard work and determination amazed her, but she worried about him, too. He pushed himself so hard.

She'd seen him start to relax, though, giving Summer this chance to decorate the cabins as well as work on the website. He'd come so far, opened up so much. With a little more time...

What? Theresa demanded of herself, derailing that thought before the train could get rolling. They'd both known going in their relationship had a quickly approaching expiration date. She was going back to St. Louis, and Jarrett had asked nothing more of her than that they spend that time together.

"He's a great guy," she told her cousin. "And we're... having fun."

"Fun?" Sophia echoed dubiously.

"Sure. What did Darcy call it? A whirlwind romance to give you married women a thrill."

"Theresa...I know you."

The words were an unspoken reminder of the conversation the two of them had had at Drew's wedding. *If you're thinking about sleeping with Jarrett, you're not falling. You're already there.*

"Maybe you knew the old me," she told her cousin. "But this is the new me. You said yourself that I've played things too safe in the past."

"I know." Sympathy and understanding shone in her cousin's dark eyes. "I just don't want to see you get hurt again."

The shop door swung open again as Summer backed out onto the sidewalk, another box in hand. "We're almost to the end of it!" she announced, and Theresa was glad to turn her attention away from her love life to finish loading the last of their purchases.

They were down to the final boxes when a young mother and her son walked by the sidewalk outside the shop.

"This is the coolest cast, doncha think, Mom?" The young boy, who Theresa guessed to be six or seven, held out the camouflaged cast encircling his wrist as if he'd just been given the best toy ever. Signs from the tears he'd shed earlier still left tracks on his slightly dirty, freckled face, but he was smiling now.

His harried-looking mother heaved a sigh as she kept a tight grip on his uninjured hand. "So cool, Bobby. About as cool as the heart attack you almost gave me jumping out of the swing like that. And do not get any ideas about a matching cast on the other wrist, okay?"

"Yeah, okay. But I can't wait for all my friends at school to see!"

Theresa smiled a little at the exchange, even as her gaze

moved down the street to the building the mother and son had exited. The small medical clinic where she, too, had had her arm set years ago. "Summer, can you handle the rest of this? There's someone I'd like to go say hello to."

The younger woman waved her off, and Theresa made her way down the sidewalk. The midafternoon sunshine held a hint of warmth, promising that spring was on the way. Four months, she realized suddenly. It had been almost four months since the accident. The agonizing days in the hospital and rehab had seemed to last forever, and yet something as everyday as squealing tires could snap her back to the nightmare of the crash as if it had happened yesterday.

Theresa took a deep breath before opening the door to the clinic. The ringing of a bell announced her arrival as she stepped inside. Warm earth tones decorated the waiting room, giving it almost a homey, more relaxed feel, unlike the various doctors' offices she'd visited in St. Louis.

"Good afternoon." Marie Oliver's eyes widened as she stepped out from the back office and saw her. "Theresa! I thought you'd gone back home with the rest of your family."

They'd bugged her about it—Alex more annoying than most of her family members—but she'd stuck with her original plan. Which was exactly what she'd told her mother when Donna called the other day to try to change her mind—again. "I'm staying through the end of the month," she told the nurse. "I was in town and just thought I'd stop by."

She wasn't sure what exactly had urged her to go to the clinic. Something about seeing that little boy. Judging by his mother's comments, it likely wasn't the first time he'd been a patient of Doc Crawford's and probably wouldn't be the last. There'd be typical injuries—scraped-up knees and palms from falling off a skateboard, maybe a busted chin. Then there would be cold and flu season throughout school years and a sports physical or two before little Bobby could play baseball or basketball. As a nurse here, Marie would be part of treating all those growing pains.

"Well, I must say you look better than the last time I saw you."

Blinking away her thoughts, Theresa glanced down at her jeans and sweatshirt. Her slightly dusty jeans and sweatshirt, as she and Summer had dug through the back storage area when Summer couldn't find just the right lamp. Unlike the cluttered but spotless front of the store, the back area was, well, even more cluttered, but not so clean. Comparing how she looked right then to the night of Debbie and Drew's wedding—

"I'm not talking about your clothes," the nurse said, following Theresa's thoughts with a smile. "I'm talking about you. You have more color in your cheeks, more spark in your eyes and even a bit of a spring in your step."

All signs of good health, Theresa thought, but also signs of great sex. She could feel a bit more color rise in her cheeks and knew she should be glad the nurse was attributing the transformation to her recovery rather than to anything else. "Well, um, thanks."

"At the wedding, your mother mentioned you'll be heading back to school soon."

Theresa sighed. "She's been encouraging me to look into hospital administration."

Marie studied her thoughtfully. "You don't sound too happy with the idea."

"It's an important job. I'm not saying otherwise, but to me, it all seems more about paperwork than patients. And it's certainly not why I became a nurse in the first place."

I want to help people. I miss helping people.

The longing had been growing steadily over the past week or so. Maybe longer than that, even as she'd disguised the need while helping out with the horses and doing a small part to help heal the rift between Jarrett and his sister. And it was something, but it wasn't enough.

Caring about people isn't something you do, it's who you are.

"But when I think of going back to the ER—the fast pace, the long hours—I just don't know if I can do it."

"It's a tough job, and I have plenty of friends who burned out working in the ER after only a few years without the injuries you sustained in the accident. How is your recovery coming?"

Talking with a fellow nurse, Theresa explained her prognosis using the medical terms she generally avoided when talking to friends and family. Naturally, she'd spoken with her own doctors and therapists, but she'd hated the role reversal of being treated like a patient. With Marie, though, she knew she was talking with an old friend and a medical professional.

"Do you mind if I take a look?" the nurse asked after Theresa explained the nerve damage she'd suffered.

"Um, no," she said, slightly surprised by the request. Holding out her arm, she allowed the nurse to check her range of motion and test her strength and flexibility. As she squeezed, she could feel the resistance of muscle and bone as her fingers closed all the way around the other woman's hand. But more than that, she could feel a returning strength in her own hand that hadn't been there weeks—even days—ago.

"Judging by the smile on your face, that's an improvement?" Marie asked as she gave a nonmedical squeeze in return.

A huge smile trembled on her lips, even as the sting

of tears burned her eyes. "I've been keeping up with my exercises, but most days, I questioned whether they were even helping. I really didn't think I was getting any better."

"Healing can be funny that way. Sometimes the steps are so small, you aren't even aware that you're taking them. But then one day, you wake up and realize just how far you've come.

"Look, I know your family is pushing you in one direction, and I don't want to pull you in another, but I'm going to say this anyway. I'm planning to retire within the next few months if not sooner. My husband took his pension last year, and the two of us want to start traveling while we're still in good enough health to do so. I've been warning Doc that he's going to have to find a replacement, but like most men, he doesn't listen to things he doesn't want to hear. But he's a good boss and great friend, so I can't just up and leave without knowing that he and all our patients are in good hands."

Opening her mouth, Theresa realized she didn't know what to say. Her first instinct was to thank the other woman for thinking of her, but as an ER nurse, she wasn't interested in working in a small-town clinic. But before she could form the words, those images of little Bobby were back and stronger than ever as she realized what working in Clearville would mean. Following patients not just through injury or illness but through their lives. Seeing them grow from an infant to a child to a teenager. Years and years from now, treating their children as Marie had had the chance to do with her cousins' families. "I—I'm sorry, but you've caught me totally off guard. I wasn't expecting this."

"Just think about it," the nurse encouraged her. "And don't worry. I won't bring it up to your family. This has to be your decision, and only you know if it's right for you to stay."

The possibilities had her head spinning as she walked out of the doctor's office. Staying in Clearville.

Staying…with Jarrett.

By the time she and Summer returned to the ranch, Theresa's head was still spinning. Was she seriously thinking about staying? What about her life in St. Louis? Her job? Her friends? She gave a small laugh at the thought. So much of her life had revolved around her job—the majority of her acquaintances centered around the ER. Not to mention her relationship with Michael.

Oh, sure, she'd had plenty of visitors while she was still in the hospital. But once she and Michael broke up, once she went home, those visits had slowed to a trickle. And she'd told herself she understood. People were busy with their own lives, but in truth, the hospital was the connection and without it, she had little else in common with her work friends.

There was Caitlyn, of course, and leaving her best friend would be hard. But with her hectic schedule at the ER, they'd already gotten used to spending more time texting and playing phone tag than seeing each other in person. Her friend would understand. Her family? Theresa sighed. She wasn't so sure how they would feel. Her mother had her heart set on Theresa going back to school, and Alex would be instantly suspicious that Theresa was changing her life for a man.

For Jarrett.

She'd tried to keep him out of the equation. She honestly did. Would she still want to move to Clearville if the two of them weren't involved? But somehow the question kept getting painfully jumbled up in her head and her heart.

Would Jarrett still want to be involved if she moved to Clearville?

They hadn't talked about the future because, up until twenty minutes ago, she wouldn't have thought they could have one. And she couldn't let it be the reason she moved halfway across the country. This kind of a life-changing decision had to be right on more levels than just their relationship alone. But that didn't mean she didn't want some sign, some reassurance, that the idea of her staying in Clearville—staying with him—would fill him with the same hope, the same sense of possibility tripping through her veins.

As Summer turned the truck onto the ranch property, Theresa asked, "Can you drop me at the stables? I'll come down to the cabin in a few minutes, but I need to talk to Jarrett first."

"Sure thing. Tell him we need his big, strong muscles for the heavy lifting if he has time."

"I'll let him know."

Her heart was pounding as she carefully lowered herself from the truck. Marie was right. She was feeling stronger, but that wasn't reason to push too hard.

Her steps faltered slightly as she approached the stable. *Pushing too hard.* She'd made that mistake with Michael. Was she about to repeat it with Jarrett? They'd known each other less than a month and now she was about to tell him that she wanted to move across country to be with him?

Oh, God, what if he didn't want her to stay?

As she stepped inside the stables, Theresa heard the sound of voices, and her steps slowed even more. Jarrett was with someone. Now wasn't the time to talk to him about her plans. Feeling as if she'd been given a reprieve, she started to turn away when he walked out of his office.

"Hey." For a second, he looked almost surprised to see

her. "I didn't think you'd be back this soon. I'm not sure if that's a good sign or not."

"What do you mean?"

"Either Summer found everything she was looking for or she ran out of money in no time flat."

"You'll have to come down to the cabin and see for yourself."

A second later, a woman in her mid-fifties appeared in the doorway, holding a cell phone. "I wasn't able to reach him, but we'll talk this evening."

Nodding to the woman, Jarrett said, "Sounds good. Let me know what you decide."

As the woman left, Theresa questioned, "Who was that?" She'd asked out of mild curiosity, but the feeling only grew when Jarrett didn't immediately answer. "Jarrett?" She followed him into his office, where he opened a cabinet drawer and pulled out a folder.

Sighing, he dropped the paperwork onto his desk. "She's a potential adopter. The work Summer's done on the website is already getting noticed."

"Well, that's great…isn't it?"

"It is. She's an experienced horsewoman, and she and her husband have plenty of acreage for a horse."

Everything he was saying sounded positive, so why did she have a growing unease in the pit of her stomach? "Okay…"

"She's interested in Silverbelle."

"Silver?" Theresa thought of the sweet, shy mare who, right along with Jarrett, had captured her heart from the first moment she'd seen the two of them ride. "But you've worked so hard with her and she's come so far—"

"Far enough that she's ready for someone to adopt her."

"I thought you were going to train her for the trail rides and riding lessons."

"That was the plan if I couldn't find someone to adopt her. Look, I know this must seem like a tough decision, but there are a few hard rules when it comes to rescue. First, you can't save them all. And second, you can't keep them all. If Silver gets adopted, I'll have room to take in another rescue. That's the way it works."

Theresa knew everything he was saying was right, so why did it all feel so wrong?

For an instant, sorrow and something else—regret? loss?—swirled in his gaze. But with a blink, the emotion was gone. "It's easier to let them go when you know they have a better life waiting for them."

"How do you know?"

"What?"

Swallowing around the sudden lump in her throat, she asked, "How do you know it's a better life?"

"I'll make sure of it. Before the final papers are signed, I'll take a ride out to their property. See that the barn and the pastures are as nice as Mrs. Davis says they are."

"Can I go with you?" Maybe Jarrett was right. Maybe seeing Silverbelle's new home would make it easier for her to accept that the little mare would be gone soon.

Jarrett froze for a moment as he reached for a pen. He wrote something on the inside of the folder as he said, "It probably won't be for another few weeks. You'll be back home by then."

Theresa sucked in a pained breath. After dancing around any mention of her departure, she felt blindsided by the sudden jab. *You'll be back home by then.* Because it would be just as easy for Jarrett to let *her* go, back to the good life she had waiting for her in St. Louis. If she'd had any hope that he would ask her to stay, he'd crushed it along with the scattered hay beneath his boots.

Tears clogged the back of her throat and burned her

eyes, but she determinedly blinked them way. Lucky for her, she wasn't one of his rescues. And she'd make up her own mind whether her future meant returning to St. Louis or making a new home in Clearville.

Chapter Fifteen

Theresa slipped from the bedroom in the early-morning light and carefully closed the door behind her. Jarrett had gone out at dawn to take care of the horses before coming back to her bed. It was a habit they'd started after the day of the storm. She'd greeted his return with open arms, feeling his chilled skin warm quickly as he slid between the sheets. Their kisses were as hungry as ever, stealing her breath as he claimed her body with his own, but she couldn't pretend anymore.

After almost two weeks of not talking about her leaving, the one mention had shattered the glass bubble around them. The outside world still existed beyond Jarrett's ranch, along with the hard decision she had yet to make.

Stay...or go?

She retreated deeper into the soft folds of her terry-cloth robe, trying to ward off a chill that came from the inside out, as she headed for the kitchen and the coffeemaker Sophia had loaned her. She went through the motions without thought, and the idea that she and Jarrett were doing the same thing—merely moving through the steps of a relationship—nearly broke her heart.

She started at a sudden knock at the front door and fought back a groan. It wouldn't be the first time one of her relatives had shown up unannounced. She wasn't necessarily trying to keep her relationship with Jarrett a secret, but that didn't mean she wanted him to waltz naked from her bedroom right into a family breakfast.

A quick glance through the window showed Summer waiting on the porch, and Theresa exhaled a small sigh of relief. It would be easy enough to tell the younger woman she'd be down to the stables in a few minutes; no reason to stick around inside her cabin.

"Summer, good morning—"

"Can I come in?" the younger woman interrupted.

"Um, I was just getting ready to head down to the stables. After I get dressed," she added, realizing she was still wearing her robe over one of Jarrett's T-shirts.

But his sister didn't seem to notice. "I just need a few minutes. Please."

The troubled look in her eyes called out to Theresa, and she simply couldn't leave Summer waiting on the porch. "Of course. I'm making some coffee if you'd like a cup?"

"Thank you."

Only after pouring them both a steaming mug of fragrant dark roast did Theresa ask, "Is everything all right?"

Staring down into her mug as if she might find the answer in the lighter swirls of cream blending with the coffee, Summer confessed, "Jarrett asked me the other day why I was really here. I guess I should have known he wouldn't believe I'd traveled all this way just to visit." She looked up as she said, "I didn't exactly tell him the truth."

Summer wrapped her hands tightly around the mug as if needing something to hold on to, something to keep her steady. "A few months ago, my mother—our mother—had a health scare. The doctors did a biopsy, and the test results came back negative, thank God."

Despite the outcome, Theresa could hear the lingering worry in the tremble in the younger woman's voice. "I'm glad everything turned out okay."

She nodded. "Me, too. But it was so hard, waiting and wondering." Emotion trembled beneath her words, drawing out more of her accent. "I wanted to call and tell Jarrett, but she wouldn't let me. She said she didn't want to bother him if it turned out to be nothing, but I don't think that was the truth. Just like I don't think she was worried about dying. Not as much as she was worried about dying without having the chance to fix what's broken between them."

Setting the mug down, she continued, "It would mean the world to my mother if Jarrett would just reach out to her. And I thought— I thought maybe you could talk to him."

"Oh, Summer..."

"He'll listen to you. I know he will. He's crazy about you. Anyone can see that."

As much as she wanted to grab hold of the younger woman's certainty, Theresa shook her head. Denying the possibility. Denying the way her heart jumped in her chest when she thought maybe, just maybe Jarrett had fallen for her the way she had for him. "I know it's tempting to get involved, but whatever problems they have, it's up to the two of them to resolve them. You and I can't fix this."

"But if you could talk him into inviting her here, I really think they'd have a chance. It's so beautiful here, so peaceful. My mother's always loved horses, and I know how proud she would be to see all Jarrett's done with the rescue, especially since she's the one who—"

Summer snapped her mouth shut suddenly, but it was clearly too late as the masculine voice demanded, "Especially after she *what*, Summer? What exactly has Lilly done that would give her *any* right to be proud of this place?"

Jarrett stepped into the kitchen, taking in the startled looks in both of their gazes. Judging by the color quickly leaching from his half sister's face, he didn't want to know whatever it was she wasn't saying. But he'd been thinking of his mother too damn often lately. First with Summer around as a painful reminder and then with talking to Theresa about his past. He should have left well enough alone.

Maybe if he hadn't talked about the past, maybe he wouldn't feel as if he was so damn close to repeating it. So damn close to having yet another woman he loved walk out on him.

Not that Theresa was to blame. He'd known all along their time together was only temporary. He should have been smart enough—strong enough—not to fall for her. But he was too like his father that way—loving a woman destined to leave.

"Jarrett, I didn't know you were— Forget it, okay? Just forget I said anything."

"No, I want to hear this. What did Lilly ever do for me other than leave me behind?"

"Jarrett—" Theresa slipped from her chair, capturing his gaze with hers. *None of this is Summer's fault. Don't take your anger out on her.*

He could read the words in her expression and was almost ready to apologize when Summer pushed away from the table, the chair legs screeching against the linoleum. "She loves you, Jarrett!"

For a split second, he had the crazy idea that she was talking about Theresa loving him, and a wild beat of hope and happiness nearly burst in his chest. But the feeling didn't last as Summer advanced on him, her normally smiling face twisted with sorrow and frustration. "All our mother has ever done is love you." Her head held high, she stared him down as she quietly asked, "Why else would she have paid the premium on your father's life insurance all those years?"

Shock sucked every bit of air from his lungs. It couldn't be true... It *couldn't* be.

"I heard Mama and Daddy arguing about it years ago. Ray started the policy when you were born, but it was Mama who paid to keep it going."

As much as he didn't want to believe Summer, it was just the kind of thing Lilly would do. The guilt that goaded her into paying for his father's care was responsible for this, too. Guilt...and pity. She'd seen that Jarrett couldn't take care of Ray when his father had needed him. Maybe she thought he'd be just as useless when it came to taking care of himself.

"I'll pay it back. Every damn dime."

"That's not what Mama wants—"

"I don't give a damn what she wants!" The words exploded from him, and Summer took a stumbling step back under their force.

Theresa wasn't so easily shaken. Instead of retreating, she moved closer. Close enough to reach out and grab his arms. Only a few hours ago, her touch had turned him inside out, but now he couldn't feel it. Couldn't feel anything. "I know this is all a huge shock, but isn't it possible that Summer's right? Can't you at least consider the possibility that your mother did this because she loves you?"

He couldn't. It was pity or guilt or, hell, maybe another

way to try to control him, but it sure as hell wasn't about love. The ranch, the rescue, everything he'd worked so hard to build as a tribute to his father had been ripped out from beneath him. The only true sense of home he'd had since he was seven yanked away just like when his mother walked out on Ray.

But he wasn't a kid anymore. And he'd be damned if he let her tear his world apart again. "Every dime," he repeated, "if it's the last thing I do."

Theresa's face paled as his words sank in. "Don't do this, Jarrett."

"Rodeo promoters are always looking for a good comeback story."

And it was the best way, the only way he could think of to make money fast. Assuming he won. But the ranch and the legacy that belonged to his *father's* blood, sweat and tears and not to his damn stepfather's easy money mattered too much for Jarrett to even think of losing.

Theresa shook her head in frustration. "I won't watch you risk your life for the sake of stupid, foolish pride!"

"You won't have to." Turning away from the sight of tears shimmering in her blue eyes, he spoke the words to the door as he reached for the handle. "You'll be back in St. Louis."

The echo of the slamming door was still resounding through the tiny cabin as Theresa sank into the kitchen chair. It was just a door, one then opened as easily as it closed, but the finality of Jarrett slamming it shut between them signaled so much more. Not just a door then, but an ending to their relationship.

A heartbreaking, devastating ending.

"Oh, Theresa! This is all my fault." Tears fell from Summer's eyes as she stared at the doorway. "I never should have said anything. I never should have come here in the first place. I wanted to help heal Jarrett's relationship with our mother and now I've made it so much worse."

A choked sob broke free, and the younger woman covered her face with her hands. Theresa's throat ached, and for a split second, she could think of nothing better than putting her head down on the table and joining Jarrett's sister. Crying her eyes out until she was too exhausted to feel the ache in her heart.

But then an old, familiar training kicked in. Caring and compassion were important aspects of nursing, but so too was being strong. Sometimes the hardest yet most important part of the job was putting emotion aside and focusing on what was best for the patient—even if it hurt.

Pushing away from the chair, Theresa walked over and pulled Summer's hands from her face. "Crying isn't going to help."

The abrupt words shocked the younger woman enough to stop, though a few hiccoughing sobs still shook her chest. "I know, but—"

"We have to figure out what will." Sucking in a deep breath, Theresa said, "I have an idea, but I'm going to need your help."

"Are you sure? You've seen what my help has done so far."

"We have to do something. He can't go back to the rodeo. If he does—" The words stopped in her throat, caught up by the lump there. "He can't go back."

She'd known for some time now that she was falling for the hardheaded rancher, but the thought of him riding again, risking injury or worse, made Theresa realize how much she loved him. How totally, completely and *hopelessly* in love she was with him.

Her heart ached with the impossibility of it all. She

loved him, and he'd just walked away. Instead of standing strong and facing this problem together, the first sign of trouble had broken them apart. But the pain didn't change how Theresa felt. And she refused to stand by while he took such a dangerous risk, not if she had even the slimmest chance to stop him.

Not even if it meant ruining any chance the two of them might have once had of being together.

Just a day or two before, Jarrett had wondered what happened to his quiet, peaceful stable. Feminine laugher had filled the place to the rafters as Theresa, Summer and Chloe had worked together, carrying on a three-way conversation he had no chance of following.

He'd done his best to stay out of the way, offering a grunt or two when one of them had thrown a question in his direction. He kept his head down, his hat pulled low in hope the brim might hide the smile he hadn't been able to keep off his face. He would have suffered through torture before admitting it, but he'd started to enjoy the energy and enthusiasm the girls brought with them. More than once, Theresa's gaze captured his with a secret smile of her own, as if she knew what he was thinking…

He didn't have to worry about blocking out their laughter today. Other than the occasional huff of breath from one of the horses, the only sound was the scrap of the shovel as he mucked out the stalls. Both Theresa and Summer had stayed away from the stables since he'd walked out of the cabin yesterday, and Chloe went about her work as quietly as possible, smart enough to know something was going on and smarter still not to ask.

Even Silverbelle seemed to be giving him the stink eye, though that was only in his imagination. It wasn't as if the little mare could know about the message from Mrs. Davis on his cell phone. The woman had talked to her husband, and the couple wanted to go through with the adoption. All Jarrett had to do was sign the papers...

"Jarrett."

The soft voice drifted through the quiet, drawing him up short as his gloved hands tightened around the wooden handle. For a split second, his brain thought it was Summer calling his name in that familiar Southern drawl. But his body knew better. His insides lurched, jerking around like that feeling of falling while caught in a nightmare. Because the voice was different—richer, mellower, more mature than his sister's.

Keeping his grip on the shovel, he backed out of the stall and looked down the length of the stable. His mother stood in the doorway, backlit by the sunlight, and dammit if it didn't *hurt* just to look at her.

Lilly Carrington always had been and always would be a beautiful woman. Her shoulder-length blond hair was perfectly styled to curl around a heart-shaped face barely touched by age. Only a few wrinkles surrounded her green eyes, and she was still as slender and graceful now as she'd been when his rawhide-tough father had fallen head over heels for her.

"I told Summer I didn't want you here."

She faced his resentment head-on, and her slender shoulders straightened beneath the cream-colored silk suit she wore. Silk in a freakin' stable. Was it any wonder his parents' marriage hadn't lasted? They were from two different worlds as different as...silk and rawhide. As night and day. As he and Theresa...

"It wasn't Summer. A young lady named Theresa called and convinced me to come."

Betrayal sliced through his gut only to be instantly cauterized by a white-hot rage. He would have expected his sister to go behind his back, but not Theresa. Not after everything he'd told her, after everything he'd shared with her about his father's stroke and what had been the worst time in his life. He swore beneath his breath. "She had no right to do that."

"She knew you'd be angry."

"Angry's not the half of it." He stalked past her as he stormed outside, but his mother followed after him, moving faster over the uneven ground in heels than he would have thought possible.

"She knew there was a chance you'd never forgive her."

She was right, dammit! He threw the shovel against the side of the stable and ripped off his gloves. And that she'd gone ahead and done it anyway—

"She took a huge risk inviting me here. Don't you think you owe it to her to at least hear what I have to say?"

"I don't owe her a damn thing." He turned the water spigot at the side of the stables on full blast and aimed the hose at the shovel. The powerful spray shot water and dirt and manure in all directions. "I've lived my life making sure I don't owe anyone. Making sure I don't end up under anyone's thumb ever again."

Keeping a safe distance, his mother spoke over the high-pitched sound of water pounding against the thin metal. "If you're talking about the life insurance—"

"The life insurance, Dad's care, the way you use George's money to control people. All of it."

"I never tried to control you."

Jarrett snorted at the flat-out lie. She wanted to talk? Fine, might as well get it over with. Anything to get her back on a plane and back in Atlanta. Hell, maybe he'd luck out and she'd take Summer with her.

Shutting off the water, he dropped the hose and turned to face her. "Never, huh? What about after Dad's stroke?

Why do you think I quit the rodeo? Why do you think I moved to Atlanta when you know how much I hated it there?"

"I thought… You wanted to be with your father."

"Yeah, I did. And I would have done it anyway, but under my terms, not because you threatened me."

He had to give her credit. Holding her head high, she looked him in the eye and quietly asked, "When did I ever threaten you, Jarrett? When did I ever ask one thing of you?" Realization dawned in her expression as she came to her own conclusion. "George," she whispered as she closed her eyes for a moment.

"Did you really think I would have gone to work for him if I'd had any other choice?"

"I had hoped…"

"Hoped that we'd be one big, happy family." Sarcasm filled his words, and he suffered a pinch of guilt when his mother flinched. Because somehow, even after everything, that really had been her hope. He knew it just as he'd known it during those court-mandated visits. But he hadn't wanted to be a part of some Brady Bunch blended family. He'd wanted his own family—the way it had been when it was just the three of them—back.

His voice was flat when he added, "George made it clear that unless I moved back and took a job at the stables, he wouldn't pay for Dad's care."

"I swear to you, Jarrett, I didn't know. And I know you think he did this as some way to punish you, but it was only because he knew how much I missed you—"

"Don't. After everything—just don't."

She looked stricken by his abrupt words. "I wish you would have told me back then."

"Why? What difference would it have made?"

"You have to know I wouldn't have held you to that bargain. I wouldn't have forced you to stay."

Right. As if she hadn't forced him to stay every summer growing up. Jarrett shook his head. "George made it all too clear. His money, his rules."

"Only it wasn't."

"Wasn't what?"

"It wasn't George's money, Jarrett. It was mine. I'm the one who paid for your father's care, and I would have continued to do so even if you'd never stepped foot in Georgia again. I know you think I married George for his money, but that's not true. I didn't need his money. I had money of my own from my side of the family."

"Since when?" he scoffed. "I remember growing up, we didn't have money. Before the divorce, I remember you and Dad fighting about it all the time."

"I'm sorry you heard those fights, but you misunderstood them. Your father always refused to touch any of my money. Even when it meant we had to struggle so hard. Even when it meant constantly moving from town to town for him to find work."

His father had always been so proud. Jarrett wasn't surprised to hear he wouldn't accept what he would have seen as a handout from Lilly's family. "Did you really think he would take money from you?"

"To save our marriage? To keep our family together? Yes, I had hoped he would. It wasn't that I expected us to live this lavish lifestyle, son. But a home of our own? A chance to put down roots and make a life for ourselves rather than all the constant moving from ranch to ranch? That's all I wanted." She spread out her hands as if to encompass the ranch, the home *he* had built, as part of the life she'd once dreamed of having. "I was in my early twenties with a young son and no support around me. I spent so many of those years feeling lonely and afraid. I needed your father, but he was gone for days and weeks at a time and when he did come home, he was exhausted from working himself half to death. All I could think was that it didn't have to be so hard. After a while, I just couldn't take it anymore."

"And so you left us."

"I left your father, Jarrett. I took you with me."

"Yeah," he snorted. "Until being a single mother got to be too hard, and you sent me back."

"You're right. It was too hard. It was too hard for me to see you so sad. You cried yourself to sleep every night! I knew how much you loved Ray and how much you would miss him, but I thought in time you'd get used to Atlanta and that visiting him would be enough. But the phone calls and visits only made it so much worse. You were miserable, and you hated living in the city. And when you started running away, I was just so afraid…"

"I was, what, seven? Eight? Every kid talks about running away when they're little."

"Not every kid makes it as far as the train station! You were ready to buy a ticket to Colorado because that's where Ray had mentioned he was living." Her shoulders slumped as she confessed, "That was the last straw. The point where I knew I couldn't win. It didn't matter what the courts may have said, I'd already lost you. You belonged with your father, and so I let you go.

"I don't expect you to believe this, but it broke my heart, Jarrett. I loved you so much and giving you up was the hardest choice I've ever had to make. Not a day goes by that I don't regret it, but I did it because I thought it was best for you. I wanted you to be happy, and I knew you'd never be happy, truly happy, if you stayed."

Her gaze pleaded with him as she added, "But I never

stopped loving you…just like I never stopped loving your father."

"You felt sorry for him and guilty for leaving. If that's what you want to call love—"

"I loved him," Lilly repeated. "And as horrible as his stroke was, it gave me a chance to do what I never could during our marriage. I finally had the chance to spend time with him and take care of him. Ray was always so strong, so independent, always keeping his emotions so tightly wrapped up inside, that he never truly let me get close. Not in the way I needed him to."

"I don't believe you." He couldn't believe her. Couldn't believe he'd been so wrong…

His mother sighed. "Well, at least believe this—the life insurance policy was never a ploy to control you. The money is yours to use with no strings attached. Don't be so foolish as to risk your life rather than accept it."

"I swore to myself after Dad's stroke that I would never take the easy way out again."

"And you are so like your father, Jarrett. Just as strong and just as stubborn. Don't you see for a man like you, accepting someone's help isn't the easy way? It's the hardest thing you could possibly do."

Chapter Sixteen

Jarrett shouldn't have been surprised Theresa tracked him down at a remote corner of his property later that afternoon. But as he looked up at the sound of hoofbeats, his heart nearly slammed to a stop when he saw her on Silver. They'd gone riding together several times since that first day, but they'd either doubled up on Champ or he'd saddled Duke and Molly for the two of them.

His muscles tightened, ready for action, as if he'd be able to catch her if she fell when she was still a dozen yards away. Even so, he couldn't help noticing she looked good in the saddle. She'd regained her confidence, and it showed in her ease of controlling the mare, in her grace, in her breathtaking beauty...

"What the hell are you thinking?" he demanded, grabbing for the reins the moment she pulled the horse to a stop beside him.

"I wanted to talk to you."

He reached for her jeans-clad hips the moment she would have tried dismounting on her own. Her breasts brushed against his chest as he lowered her to the ground, and he gritted his teeth against the impossible longing. He held her for a moment longer than necessary, his body refusing to obey his brain as muscle memory took over. How many times had he reached for her during the past two weeks? In bed and out? He didn't want to let her go. *Not now, not ever.*

He dropped his arms and forced himself to step back quickly before he could think of the pain to come. Ripping off the bandage and leaving tattered pieces of his heart behind. "You could have driven."

"I wanted to ride."

"Silver?"

She tossed her dark ponytail back over one shoulder. "Why not? You said yourself she's ready for adoption."

"Yes! By an experienced horsewoman!"

Her eyebrows rose in challenge, and he gave up the argument. Silver was ready, but so, too, was Theresa. It was time for them both to move on.

He turned back to the final section of decrepit fencing he had yet to dismantle. He could have spent the time working on one of the cabins, but he was not in the right state of mind to build something. Tearing stuff down with his bare hands? Yeah, that better suited his mood.

He had half a dozen boards in the back of the truck already, and he tossed another piece into the bed, where it landed with a satisfying thud. Two more boards followed, and Theresa had yet to say a word. He made a show of focusing on the job at hand, wrenching the sagging crossbeams from the rotting posts. The wood gave way from rusty metal with a nails-against-chalkboard screech. Despite the mild temperature, sweat stung his eyes, but he didn't stop to wipe it away.

The heat from the sun was nothing compared to the magnifying-glass intensity of Theresa's gaze, and finally he couldn't take it anymore. He threw the crowbar into the back of the truck with a loud clatter and stripped off his gloves. "You want to talk? Talk. You can start by telling me what the hell you thought you were doing by inviting my mother to come here."

"I thought you needed to hear her side of the story."

Ever since talking to his mother, images from the past had played through his mind like a movie he'd seen a dozen times, only now, he was wearing the 3-D glasses he'd never had before. Subtle nuances he'd missed stood out, sharp and clear and cutting.

His excitement as a little boy for his dad coming home... because Ray had been gone for weeks at a time.

The awesome forts he'd made out of cardboard boxes... after they'd moved again and again and again.

A childhood filled with freedom for him...and a marriage filled with loneliness for his mother.

And now, everything he had, everything he'd spent the past two years building in his father's name—the ranch, the rescue, his chance for a life after the rodeo—he owed to his mother. The solid future he'd built for himself suddenly seemed as shaky as the rotting fence, ready to collapse with one good shove.

He felt hollowed out inside, empty and...scared. Just as he had as a little kid when his mother took him away from his father, from the ranch and the horses and the land that he'd already loved.

He hated the raw vulnerability as the pride he'd taken in all he'd accomplished was stripped away, leaving him naked, bleeding and exposed... With Theresa there to witness the humiliation.

"You shouldn't have asked her to come here. You had no right—"

"Right?" She interrupted, her blue eyes flashing, her ponytail trembling with the emotion surging through her. "I think I have every right to do whatever it takes to keep you from getting yourself killed!"

"You don't know—"

"And neither do you! You said yourself one throw from a bull could be all that it takes, and yet you're willing to take that chance? Why? Why is it so hard for you to see that your mother loves you?"

Jarrett flinched as her words reached out and slapped at him. Lilly had told him accepting help was that hardest thing for him to do, but she was wrong. Accepting love was. Accepting it, believing it, counting on it only to find one day that it was gone.

Theresa stepped closer, her anger softening around the edges, but her body still strung tight from holding back the tide of emotion. And he knew what she was going to say. Saw it written in the gorgeous sapphire of her eyes.

"*I* love you, Jarrett. I want to stay here. I want to be with you, but not if you go back to bull riding. Not if you're willing to risk your life rather than—rather than risking your heart." The tears welling in her eyes reached the breaking point, spilling over her lashes and down her cheeks. "All you have to do is ask me to stay."

Don't go. Stay.

As the words repeated through his head, Jarrett realized why they sounded so heartbreakingly familiar. He'd heard them before—the last words his father spoke to his mother before she left him.

Don't go. Stay.

He'd only been seven at the time, but even at that young age, he'd heard the sheer desperation, the utter hopelessness behind them. He'd known then, just as he knew now, that they wouldn't be enough.

So he did what his father hadn't been able to and remained silent as the woman he loved left him behind.

Tears blinded Theresa on the ride back to the stables, turning the rolling hills and green meadows into a shimmering watercolor painting. She was lucky Silver was so well trained that the mare knew her way home. But when she thought of Jarrett giving the horse up, sending her away from the only home she'd likely known, the tears only fell faster. Ragged sobs built in her chest, but she held them back until she reached the corral. Sliding from the saddle, she buried her face against the satiny warmth of Silver's neck.

She loved him so much, and for a split second, she'd fooled herself into thinking he might feel the same. She'd known inviting his mother to the ranch was a risk, and she'd expected his anger. What she saw, though, as he'd first caught sight of her astride Silver was a concern that overwhelmed everything else. His hazel eyes had widened, and when he pulled her into his arms, she'd felt the shaky breath he took, the longing that reached inside her, caught hold of her heart and sparked a rhythm loud enough that he surely must have been able to hear it. *Don't let go. Don't let go.*

But he'd done more than let her go. He'd pushed her away. She'd poured out her heart and soul, and he'd left them bleeding on the ground. And as hurt as she was, as angry as she was, she was more terrified than anything. If Jarrett went back to bull riding, all it would take was one wrong move. One bad fall…

Theresa didn't know how long she stood there, taking what comfort she could from the patient mare's solid presence, before old habits kicked in. She took her time unsaddling the horse, brushing her down and seeing that she had fresh water and a few extra pieces of carrot before stabling her.

"I guess I don't need to ask how things went."

Summer's soft voice reached Theresa as she gave Silver a final pat. *I'm going to miss you, girl.*

Taking a deep breath, she faced Jarrett's sister. "I knew the chance I was taking."

Summer's eyes—so similar to Jarrett's—filled with tears. "This is all my fault. If I hadn't come here, none of this would have happened."

"Don't blame yourself, Summer. You were trying to reunite your family and only had Jarrett's best interests at heart. I know that, and I—I can only hope he'll get that through his thick skull and figure it out for himself."

But it was a realization he'd have to make on his own because he'd been right about one thing. It was time for her to go.

Stars still hung in the inky sky when Jarrett walked down to the stables. He'd given up sleeping sometime around four o'clock that morning. About twenty minutes later, he gave up eating as he couldn't stomach more than a bite or two of the bacon and eggs he'd fried.

Hunching into his denim jacket against the chill in the air, his hat pulled low, he almost missed seeing the shadowed figure leaning against the corral fence. Even in the faint light, his mother's blond hair gleamed. His footsteps slowed, but it was too late. She whirled at the crunch of his boot heels on the gravel path, clutching the blanket she'd draped over her shoulders closer to her chest. "Oh, goodness, Jarrett." Her breath escaped in a cloud as she gasped. "You startled me. I didn't expect you to be up this early."

Not bothering to explain that "out late" would have been a better description than "up early," he shrugged. "Could say the same about you."

Opening the door to the stables, he flicked on the light in his small office. The chores could wait until the sun at least peeked over the horizon, but there was always paperwork to do. Mostly because he always put it off for as long as possible. If nothing else, maybe the tediousness of it all would help him find the sleep that had eluded him.

Lilly trailed after him, hitching up the blanket to keep the corner from dragging on the ground behind her. "Yes, well, I don't want to bother you, but I wanted you to know I'll be checking in to a hotel in town for the rest of my stay."

The harsh lighting touched on her resigned expression. Maybe it was the early-morning hour, the bed-rumpled hair and lack of makeup, but Lilly looked pale and tired. She held her head high, though, managing a small smile as she said, "I'm sure ya'll will be glad to have us out of your hair."

"'Us?'" he echoed, a little surprised that Summer would be making the move to town, even though it only made sense.

"Yes, I spoke with Summer. She says Theresa's leaving today, too."

He froze as he circled around his desk. Two days. They were still supposed to have two days, and even after all that had happened, he didn't want her to leave. He wanted those two days of torturing himself with her presence before sinking into a lifetime of torturing himself with her absence.

Pulling out his chair, he dropped into the seat. Ten

years' worth of bone-jarring rides and backbreaking falls caught up with him, and he ached from head to toe. Even his teeth seemed to hurt as he forced the words out. "It's probably for the best."

"Best for whom? Certainly not you if your appearance is anything to go by. You look horrible." Concern filled her eyes as she asked, "Did you sleep at all?"

Don't worry about that nasty nightmare. I'm right here...

"Doesn't matter," he said abruptly. "It's like you said. Sometimes loving means letting go, and I—I just want what's best for Theresa."

His mother stared at him, her jaw going slightly slack. "Of all the things we talked about, that's the one thing you take to heart? Honestly, J.T...."

He waited for the quick stab of pain at hearing his childhood nickname spoken in that soft, Southern drawl, but it didn't come. Maybe he was just too wrung out to feel much of anything.

But as his mother stepped closer, reaching out a tentative hand from beneath the blanket to touch his shoulder, the numbness inside his chest started to wear off a bit. "Sending you back to your father was the hardest decision I ever had to make. As your mother, I had to put my own feelings aside and do what was best for my little boy.

"But, Jarrett, Theresa isn't a child. She's a grown woman. She doesn't need you to decide what's best for her. She can make up her own mind, and if you give her half the chance, she'll choose you. That girl loves you, and if you let her go, you'll regret it. Just like I've spent my life regretting losing you."

As feeling rushed back to his heart, pinpricks of awareness jabbing like thousands of needles, Jarrett thought maybe the numbness was better. He wanted to retreat back into the unfeeling shell where nothing could reach him. Untouched…unloved.

Lilly's hand slowly slipped away, disappointment written in her expression as she headed toward the office door. She'd taken a step outside before he asked, "How long are you staying in town?"

"Until the end of the week."

"Okay. I, uh, I'll see you."

As promises went, it wasn't much. But as their gazes met, the hope in his mother's eyes told him she recognized that it was something at least. A place to start. "Okay, then, I'll see you later."

Jarrett didn't know how long he sat alone after she left, staring blankly at the top of his desk before a folder caught his eye. Silverbelle's paperwork. He'd pulled it out the other day after the potential adopter stopped by. The file contained everything from Mrs. Davis's adoption application to vet records to the recent photos Summer had taken for the rescue website. But as he flipped the folder open, the picture that slid out wasn't one of Summer's.

It was the shot he'd taken the day Silver arrived.

He would never claim to have his sister's gift for capturing a horse's spirit and personality in a single snap, but his lack of skill wasn't the problem. Not even a world-class photographer could have made that picture into anything more than it was—a heartbreaking image of a mistreated animal.

If Jarrett didn't know better, he would swear it wasn't the same horse. Little more than skin and bones, Silver's lackluster eyes gazed back at the camera. She'd been in bad shape, neglected and abused and wary of any person who got within ten feet of her.

On Theresa's first day at the ranch, he'd thought he'd seen something in her blue eyes that reminded him of Silver's soft brown ones. But looking at the horse as she'd been when she first arrived, Jarrett didn't see Theresa at all.

He saw himself.

Beaten and broken and distrustful of anyone who tried to reach out, even with a helping hand. And like Silver in those early days, he snapped and kicked and warned them all to keep their distance.

But unlike Silver, who'd bravely gone on to trust in humans again, he'd given up. Oh, he'd healed on the outside, but inside? The pain of the past still festered, and when anyone got too close—his mother, his sister, Theresa—he'd lashed out.

He rubbed at the ache in his chest. He'd thought he was playing it safe. After all, what kind of idiot put his heart out there time and again only to have it trampled over and over? So he'd kept his guard up, but what he'd been protecting wasn't worth having. Bitterness, anger, resentment, he'd held on to it all, unwilling to give it up, unwilling to let it go.

If his work with rescue horses had taught him anything over the past year, it was that the first step was always the hardest. Once an animal took that chance, once it started moving forward and not looking back, he knew the slow road to recovery would begin. All it took was a first step.

Reaching out, he picked up the phone and dialed the number on the adoption application.

Did it make her a coward, Theresa wondered, that she'd stopped by the ranch's small rental office to drop off her key rather than going out to the stables? She'd known her chances of seeing Jarrett were slim, and the relief pouring through her when she stepped inside the empty room nearly left her light-headed.

She placed the envelope on the desk. She'd thought about leaving a note, but her courage had failed her there, too. She'd been afraid of what she might write.

I love you, Jarrett. I want to stay here. I want to be with you. Please. All you have to do is ask.

But she already knew how that played out. She'd never heard a sound as loud as Jarrett's heartbreaking silence. Without any response from him, her own words played like an endless record through her thoughts—more painful, more humiliating with every turn.

It would get better, she promised herself. Given enough time, she would start to heal, and the pain would begin to fade. But her love for Jarrett? That would stay with her for a long, long time.

Blinking back tears, she stepped out of the office, and her heart nearly stopped when she caught sight of him seated on Silverbelle just a few yards away. Just like the first time she'd seen him on the horse, he took her breath away. He sat strong and sure in the saddle, his hat pulled low over his brow, but she could still feel the intensity of his green-gold gaze.

"Theresa…"

The low murmur of her name on his lips seeped into her soul.

After all that silence, had he really sought her out just to say goodbye?

Swinging down from the saddle, he walked toward the porch and paused with his boot on the first step. Déjà vu swept over her, a replay from that first moment all those weeks ago. She'd been standing in that same spot, her luggage beside her, after her cousin had dropped her off. And now she was there again, waiting for Sophia to pick her up.

Two brief moments of welcome and farewell bookending what felt like a lifetime in between.

"Don't go. Stay."

The breath she didn't realize she'd been holding whooshed from her lungs. *Not goodbye after all...* Her heart fluttered in her chest. Tiny signs of life to prove it was bruised but not broken.

"Jarrett..."

"Don't go back to St. Louis."

St. Louis. Theresa could have told him right then about her plans, about her decision to stay. About the tour Marie Oliver had given her of the medical clinic. About meeting with Doc Crawford and instantly liking the older man's calm, caring demeanor, his confidence in her abilities. About how stepping into the exam rooms had felt so *right*, and she'd known it was the place for her.

A nursing career in a small town would never be the same high-energy, fast-paced adrenaline rush of working in an inner-city emergency room. But the local clinic would give her an opportunity the ER never had—the chance to slow down and truly get to know her patients. To learn more about them than whatever immediate injury needed treatment. To help over the long run rather than focusing on the short-term.

And she had hoped, too, that sticking around would prove to Jarrett that she was there to stay. She'd make her own decisions about what was best for her and her future. But she wasn't ready to let him off the hook so soon. Not when there was still so much undecided. "I told you, I won't watch you risk your life bull riding again."

"About that...I called a rodeo promoter. A friend from the old days."

Fear sliced through her. "No, Jarrett. Please."

"I talked to him about having a benefit rodeo at the Clearville fairgrounds with the proceeds going toward the rescue."

"You…what?" The words, so different from the ones she'd expected, almost didn't register as Jarrett finished the climb up the porch steps and stopped in front of her. Her gaze roved over his handsome face as she tried to make sense of what he was saying.

Different words…different man.

The shadows were gone from his eyes. The air of isolation around him had disappeared. He looked younger, free from the burdens of the past.

"From there, the ball just kept rolling as I got in touch with some old friends and sponsors."

It hadn't been easy to make those calls. Asking favors from people he hadn't talked to in over a year. He still felt humbled and slightly ashamed at the warm responses he'd received. Their willingness to hear what he had to say only emphasized the realization he'd had. If his friends had walked away from him after his injury, it was only because he'd repeatedly shoved them out the door.

"It's gonna be a huge undertaking and hard to say how much money it'll bring in the first year…" Jarrett shrugged, trying to focus on realistic expectations and not let his excitement carry him away.

"I think it sounds like a great idea. The perfect way for you to bring attention to the rescue." She hesitated a second before quietly adding, "You know your mother doesn't want you to pay her back, don't you?"

"I know, but I need to. And I've talked to her about it. We've both decided the money was a loan, and I'll pay it off as I can. Both she and Summer are over-the-top excited about the rodeo."

"You're letting them help?"

"Letting them?" he echoed with a laugh. "I don't think I could stop them. And I'd be stupid to try. I might know rodeos, but I don't have a clue when it comes to charity events. My mother has made a career out of volunteering and raising money for charities. And even if she hadn't, it feels right to do this together. I think—I think it's what my dad would have wanted."

"And you?"

"I want this, too. I've spent too many years of my life thinking I was better off on my own. I didn't need anyone, and I didn't want anyone to need me. I thought that meant I was tough, but all it really meant was that I was afraid of letting anyone too close. Until I met you."

Tears shimmered in her eyes, and a sudden panic gripped his chest, but he pushed past the nerves, past the fear. "I love you, Theresa. I should have told you that yesterday. Hell, I should have told you that weeks ago. And if I haven't ruined everything by being a hardheaded fool, then I'd like a second chance to do this right."

He yanked his hat off his head, spinning the brim between his palms to keep his hands occupied. To keep from reaching out, pulling Theresa into his arms and telling her with his body everything he wanted to say. She needed the words, the ones he'd denied when she'd poured her heart out and he'd kept silent.

"I love you, too. Stay. Please stay. I can't imagine my life without you."

The tears she'd been holding back spilled over her cheeks. "I'm not going anywhere, cowboy."

"But I thought—"

"I need to go to St. Louis to pack my things, but then I'm coming back here. In a few months, I'm taking over for the nurse at Doc Crawford's office. I'll have a chance to get to know patients as people, as my neighbors. From now on, this is my home, too."

Her words lifted a weight from his chest, but deep down, Jarrett knew it wouldn't have mattered. If Theresa had moved back to St. Louis…he didn't know what it would be like to run a horse rescue in the city, but he would have found out.

"I never should have tried to push you away."

"What about Silver?"

Jarrett looked over at the mare. Maybe it was just imagination that the horse seemed to cock her head in their direction, flicking her ears as if waiting for his answer, but he smiled anyway. "Don't worry, girl," he called out. "You're staying here. Right where you belong."

"Right where *we* belong," Theresa corrected.

Hearing the certainty in her words, the promise of forever, Jarrett knew it was true. "Where we belong," he echoed as he leaned forward and sealed the words with a kiss.

Clearville might be where he lived, but Theresa was his home.

* * * * *

Don't miss Ryder Kincaid's story,
HIS SECRET SON
the next installment in Stacy Connelly's miniseries
THE PIRELLI BROTHERS

On sale April 2015,
wherever Harlequin books are sold!

REQUEST YOUR FREE BOOKS!
2 FREE NOVELS PLUS 2 FREE GIFTS!

♥ HARLEQUIN®

SPECIAL EDITION
Life, Love & Family

YES! Please send me 2 FREE Harlequin® Special Edition novels and my 2 FREE gifts (gifts are worth about $10). After receiving them, if I don't wish to receive any more books, I can return the shipping statement marked "cancel." If I don't cancel, I will receive 6 brand-new novels every month and be billed just $4.74 per book in the U.S. or $5.24 per book in Canada. That's a savings of at least 14% off the cover price! It's quite a bargain! Shipping and handling is just 50¢ per book in the U.S. and 75¢ per book in Canada.* I understand that accepting the 2 free books and gifts places me under no obligation to buy anything. I can always return a shipment and cancel at any time. Even if I never buy another book, the two free books and gifts are mine to keep forever.

235/335 HDN F45Y

Name	(PLEASE PRINT)

Address	Apt. #

City	State/Prov.	Zip/Postal Code

Signature (if under 18, a parent or guardian must sign)

Mail to the **Harlequin® Reader Service:**
IN U.S.A.: P.O. Box 1867, Buffalo, NY 14240-1867
IN CANADA: P.O. Box 609, Fort Erie, Ontario L2A 5X3

Want to try two free books from another line?
Call 1-800-873-8635 or visit www.ReaderService.com.

* Terms and prices subject to change without notice. Prices do not include applicable taxes. Sales tax applicable in N.Y. Canadian residents will be charged applicable taxes. Offer not valid in Quebec. This offer is limited to one order per household. Not valid for current subscribers to Harlequin Special Edition books. All orders subject to credit approval. Credit or debit balances in a customer's account(s) may be offset by any other outstanding balance owed by or to the customer. Please allow 4 to 6 weeks for delivery. Offer available while quantities last.

Your Privacy—The Harlequin® Reader Service is committed to protecting your privacy. Our Privacy Policy is available online at www.ReaderService.com or upon request from the Harlequin Reader Service.

We make a portion of our mailing list available to reputable third parties that offer products we believe may interest you. If you prefer that we not exchange your name with third parties, or if you wish to clarify or modify your communication preferences, please visit us at www.ReaderService.com/consumerchoice or write to us at Harlequin Reader Service Preference Service, P.O. Box 9062, Buffalo, NY 14269. Include your complete name and address.

HSE13R

SPECIAL EXCERPT FROM

H HARLEQUIN®

SPECIAL EDITION

*Newly promoted Nathan Garrett is eager to prove he's no
longer the company playboy. His assistant, single mom
Allison Caldwell, has no interest in helping him with that
goal, despite the fiery attraction between them. But as
Nate grows closer to Alli's little boy, she wonders whether
he might be a family man after all...*

*Read on for a sneak preview of THE DADDY WISH,
by award-winning author Brenda Harlen, the next book in
the miniseries THOSE ENGAGING GARRETTS!*

***

Allison sipped her wine. Dammit—her pulse was racing
and her knees were weak, and there was no way she could
sit here beside Nate Garrett, sharing a drink and conversation, and not think about the fact that her tongue had tangled
with his.

"I think I'm going to call it a night."

"You haven't finished your wine," he pointed out.

"I'm not much of a drinker."

"Stay," he said.

She lifted her brows. "I don't take orders from you outside
the office, Mr. Garrett."

"Sorry—your insistence on calling me 'Mr. Garrett' made
me forget that we weren't at the office," he told her. "Please,
will you keep me company for a little while?"

"I'm sure there are any number of other women here who
will happily keep you company when I'm gone."

"I don't want anyone else's company," he told her.

"Mr. Garrett—"

"Nate."

She sighed. "Why?"

"Because it's my name."

"I meant, why do you want my company?"

"Because I like you," he said simply.

"You don't even know me."

His gaze skimmed down to her mouth, lingered, and she knew he was thinking about the kiss they'd shared. The kiss she hadn't been able to stop thinking about.

"So give me a chance to get to know you," he suggested.

"You'll have that chance when you're in the VP of Finance's office."

She frowned as the bartender, her friend Chelsea, slid a plate of pita bread and spinach dip onto the bar in front of her. "I didn't order this."

"But you want it," Chelsea said, and the wink that followed suggested she was referring to more than the appetizer.

"Actually, I want my bill. It's getting late and…" But her friend had already turned away.

Allison was tempted to walk out and leave Chelsea to pick up the tab, but the small salad she'd made for her own dinner was a distant memory, and she had no willpower when it came to three-cheese spinach dip.

She blew out a breath and picked up a grilled pita triangle. "The service here sucks."

"I've always found that the company of a beautiful woman makes up for many deficiencies."

***

Don't miss THE DADDY WISH by award-winning author Brenda Harlen, the next book in her new miniseries, **THOSE ENGAGING GARRETTS!** *Available February 2015, wherever Harlequin® Special Edition books and ebooks are sold.*
www.Harlequin.com

HARLEQUIN®

A Romance FOR EVERY MOOD™

Stay up-to-date on all your
romance-reading news with the
Harlequin Shopping Guide,
featuring bestselling authors, exciting new
miniseries, books to watch and more!

The newest issue will be delivered right to you
with our compliments! There are 4 each year.

Signing up is easy.

EMAIL

ShoppingGuide@Harlequin.ca

WRITE TO US

HARLEQUIN BOOKS
Attention: Customer Service Department
P.O. Box 9057, Buffalo, NY 14269-9057

OR PHONE

1-800-873-8635 in the United States
1-888-343-9777 in Canada

Please allow 4-6 weeks for delivery of the first issue by mail.

HARLEQUIN®

A *Romance* FOR EVERY MOOD™

JUST CAN'T GET ENOUGH?

Join our social communities
and talk to us online.

You will have access to the latest
news on upcoming titles and special
promotions, but most importantly,
you can talk to other fans about your
favorite Harlequin reads.

Harlequin.com/Community

 Facebook.com/HarlequinBooks

 Twitter.com/HarlequinBooks

Pinterest.com/HarlequinBooks

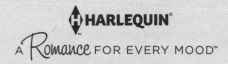